谨以此书献给十七年前因癌症故去的妻子郑珊芬

Dedicated to my deceased wife, Zheng Shanfen

Who died of cancer seventeen years ago

众里寻他千百度

中国爱情诗词选译

◉黄遵洸 译注

浙江工商大学出版社
—杭州

图书在版编目(CIP)数据

众里寻他千百度:中国爱情诗词选译:汉英对照 / 黄遵洮译注. —杭州:浙江工商大学出版社,2020.4
ISBN 978-7-5178-3763-3

Ⅰ. ①众… Ⅱ. ①黄… Ⅲ. ①古典诗歌—诗集—中国—汉、英 Ⅳ. ①I222

中国版本图书馆 CIP 数据核字(2020)第028238号

众里寻他千百度:中国爱情诗词选译
ZHONGLI XUN TA QIANBAIDU: ZHONGGUO AIQING SHICI XUANYI
黄遵洮 译注

出 品 人	鲍观明
策划编辑	沈 娴
责任编辑	沈 娴
责任校对	刘 颖 费一琛
封面设计	王好驰
责任印制	包建辉
出版发行	浙江工商大学出版社 (杭州市教工路198号 邮政编码310012) (E-mail:zjgsupress@163.com) (网址:http://www.zjgsupress.com) 电话:0571-88904980,88831806(传真)
排 版	杭州朝曦图文设计有限公司
印 刷	杭州高腾印务有限公司
开 本	880mm×1230mm 1/32
印 张	6.625
字 数	120千
版 印 次	2020年4月第1版 2020年4月第1次印刷
书 号	ISBN 978-7-5178-3763-3
定 价	58.00元

Acknowlegements

The author thanks all those who have helped to make the publication of this book successful. Among them, he is much grateful to his former teacher, Prof. Ren Shaozeng, who generously encouraged the author in his construction of the book's general theme and arrangement. Thanks to Luo Zijiang, Nisheng Wenxin, his former school mates, who gave their precious suggestions for revision. Lastly, he is also indebted to Miss Shen Xian, editor in charge of the book, whose hard work is the determined factor of making this a better book.

Preface

This select collection is specially prepared for the international students now studying in the universities in China, who are much interested in Chinese literature, especially Chinese classical poetry. As the author of the book, I may probably be asked why love is designed for the very theme of this collection. It is quite obvious that young people (university students) are more concerned about love than the other age groups, for they are in the prime of life, and more attracted to the opposite sex. And as a result, love poems enjoy more readers in this group than in any other reading groups.

Love, especially love between both sexes, is one of the basic affections in human life, and therefore, it is called by many people, "the crown of life". In different periods of human life, love may be shown in quite different forms of expression, i. e. ignorance or anxiety in first love, thrill at a glimpse of an enchanting beauty or a handsome man, disappointment of missing the chance of meeting one's beloved, affection for husband or wife, lament of separation of couples between life and death, and condolence of blood and tears on the deceased husband or wife, etc. All these affections are vividly and clearly expressed in the Chinese classical love poems, and the affections are deep, mild and moderate, never expressed in exceeding ways, whereas in the western love poems, poets tend to be direct, bold, and passionate.

Chinese love poems have a long history, which can be traced back to the love poem *Guanju* (*Fish Eagles*), the opening selected poem in *The Book of Songs*, the first collection of classical Chinese poems. About *Guanju*, Confucius says, "*The Kwan Tsü* is expressive of enjoyment without being licentious, and of grief without being hurtfully excessive" (translated by James Legge). In a sense, he recommends *Fish Eagles* as the model of Chinese love poems. And moreover, Confucius stresses that love between both sexes should naturally lead to marriage. In his opinion, marriage is the foundation of a family, and harmonious families are the reliable guarantee to a peaceful and civilized society, and a stable and flourishing society helps the country become peaceful and prosperous. Themes of Chinese classical poems including love play a very important role in the molding of the spirit and disposition of the Chinese people. To read more Chinese love poems can help foreign friends know more of the inner world of the Chinese people. It is, therefore, our sacred historical responsibility to introduce our splendid Chinese classical poems to people all over the world.

To translate poems (Chinese—English) is no easy job even though translation practice has a history of two hundred years or so (the first introduction of Chinese poems to Western readers by Peter Perring, *The Flower Leaf: Chinese Courtship in Verse*, in London, 1824). Regretfully, the translator Peter Perring, probably a China expert, yet not bred in the background of Chinese culture, would have met with lots of difficulties in his comprehension of the Chinese poems, and therefore, his translation is not perfect enough compared with any other versions by the Chinese translators hereafter. Since 1949, China has cultivated lots of translators in different languages, and some of them are of international fame, such as Xu Yuanchong, Yang Xianyi, Bian Zhilin. And Mr. Xu is perhaps the best known, who has not only published many classical Chinese poems in English and in French but also established his theory of re-creation in literary translation.

To my mind, the first step towards the successful rendering of a poetic work is the full comprehension of the source text, especially the mood (意境) of the whole work. Take *A Message* (《寄人》:别梦依依到谢家,小廊回合曲阑斜。多情只有春庭月,犹为离人照落花。) by the Tang poet Zhang Bi (张泌) for example. It is a poem expressing a hero's grief and regret after the separation from his love. My translation is as follows:

Since our separation I have often dreamed as if I were in your residence,

Where the veranda was winding, and the balustrade slanting as ever.

In the yard the spring moon seemed to be the only thing affectionate and tender,

Which was shedding light on the fallen petals for my love's absence.

In the English version, as a whole, I employ these words or images to produce the mood or literary atmosphere of the source text: "as if" for "依依"; "Where the veranda was winding, and the balustrade slanting as ever" indicates "things were still there, but his love was no longer seen"; "the spring moon seemed to be the only thing affectionate and tender" implys that his absent love was less affectionate and tender than the spring moon which was still shedding light on the fallen petals for her, his beloved; the word "shed" suggests "shedding tears", and "the fallen petals" stands for the youthful days having gone by, yet only the moon light still remembered the absent love and their past love stories. I have done everything possible to help contribute to the production of the mood in the poem.

"Mood or literary atmosphere"(意境) is the unique term put forward by the forerunners of poetic criticism in our Chinese poetical theory, whereas in the Western poetical theoretical works, the corresponding word is "vision". "Mood" and "vision" are quite different words no matter in meaning or in suggestion. Then, what is mood? In traditional Chinese poetical theory, "mood" is a successful blend of scenery and the sentiment of the poet (i. e. the artistic state created by objective images and the poet's personal affections). Mood plays a very important role in the composition of any poem. Wang Guowei, a great scholar and well-known critic of Ci poetry, says, the most important factor in writing a good Ci poem is how to successfully produce its mood. And in the process of translating a poem, we should always keep in mind that we must try every possible way to make all the words, images and rhymes contribute to the creation of mood.

Strictly, it is impossible to clone a poem into another language. Just as Robert Frost says, poetry is what gets lost in translation. What he says suggests that he doubts the translatability of poems, for it seems to him that in the process of rendering a poem into another language, it is quite probable to lose a few things of the original in its sense and form. Take the rendering of sense for example. Sense, in the main, is expressed by the use of words. According to the Chinese traditional poetical theory, the words used in poetry composition can be divided into several kinds, i.e. words with double meanings (唐代刘禹锡《竹枝词》"东边日出西边雨,道是无晴却有晴", in which the word "晴" indicates "情",

love), words with charm (唐代张泌《寄人》"多情只有春庭月,犹为离人照落花", in which the poet seemingly praises the moon, actually he's murmuring complaints for the hero), symbolic words (晋代陶渊明《饮酒(其五)》"采菊东篱下,悠然见南山", in which "菊""东篱""南山" with the meaning chrysanthemums, eastern fence, southern mountains respectively, symbolize the poet's life in seclusion), words with deeper implications (北宋欧阳修《蝶恋花(庭院深深深几许)》"泪眼问花花不语,乱红飞过秋千去", which means in tears, the hero asks the flowers why, but they keep silence, and instead of answering the hero, they fly over the swing in a riot of petals. Here, the meaning goes deeper forward from one layer into another), etc. In a word, the use of words plays a very important role in creating the mood of a poem.

Another important factor is the employment of imagery. Imagery means the vivid, perceived poetic images created with imagination, vision and figures of speech by the poet. In our Chinese classical poems, a life of staying away from home (羁旅) is a very often seen topic for poets. For instance, in the Tang poet Wen Tingyun's *An Early Start in Mount Shang* (唐代温庭筠《商山早行》), the poet depicts the travel-worn life and home-sickness of a traveler. The top half of the poem runs like this: "晨起动征铎,客行悲故乡。鸡声茅店月,人迹板桥霜。" (The bell is urging us an early start in the morn; / As a traveler I feel rather homesick and worn. / Under the setting moon a cock crows in the hut; / On the wooden bridge foot-prints in frost are seen.) The third and fourth lines are antithetical, which are composed of at least six isolated images without any verbs and conjunctions. The moon, the crowing cock, the hut, the wooden bridge, the foot-prints and the frost are all images which contribute to producing the mood in which the traveler is both worn out and homesick. I don't think such a way of using imagery could be found in the writings of the Western poets.

Lastly, the use of form. China is a great country of poetry in the world, with a long history of poem writing, and it has developed various kinds of forms of poetry since the publication of *The Book of Songs*, i.e. songs of Chu, Yuefu ballads, five-character poems of Wei and Jin Dynasties, Tang poems, Ci poems of Song, Sanqu of Yuan, and vernacular verses. As a result, it is very difficult or rather impossible to "transplant" the forms of Chinese poetry into any other languages. Naturally, in my translation in this collection I almost neglect the reproduction of forms into the English versions. With a sober mind, I've never tried to achieve likeness in form. If possible, I only have attempted to use end rhyme, without spoiling the sense of the source text.

It is my first trial on the rendering of the classical Chinese poems into English, so errors and mistakes are probable and unavoidable because of my poor mastery of both Chinese and English. Sincerely and honestly, I hope experts and the other readers will not hesitate to point them out. Criticism is always welcome.

目录
Contents

附：现代爱情诗歌

Appendix: Modern Love Poems

众里寻他千百度

关　雎

选自先秦《诗经·周南》

关关①雎鸠，
在河之洲。
窈窕淑女，
君子好逑②。

参差荇菜③，
左右流之，
窈窕淑女，
寤寐④求之。

Fish Eagles

Selected from *Zhounan*, *The Book of Songs* in the Pre-Qin Period

"Guan-guan!" cry the fish eagles
Seeking company on the river isles.
Behold that fair and sweet maiden,
Who's the fit mate for a good swain.

Long and short duckweed groves
Should be gathered by all means;
That sweet and graceful maiden
Is always in the heart of a good swain.

求之不得，
寤寐思服[5]。
悠哉悠哉，
辗转反侧。

参差荇菜，
左右采之。
窈窕淑女，
琴瑟友之。

参差荇菜，
左右芼[6]之。
窈窕淑女，
钟鼓乐之。

Having failed in getting her,

He is day and night missing her.

It is for her so profound a longing

That he is in bed all night tossing.

Long and short duckweed groves

Should be picked by all means.

As for that sweet and fair maiden,

He should get close to her by musical means.

Long and short duckweed groves

Should be plucked by all means.

As for that sweet and fair maiden,

He should please her with bells and drums.

注释：

①关关：象声调，鸟鸣声，此处是雎鸠（一种类似鱼鹰的水鸟）的叫声。

②逑：配偶。

③荇菜：一种水生植物，可食用。

④寤寐：醒来和睡着。

⑤思服：思念。

⑥芼：采摘。上文中的“流”和“采”跟它同一意思。

解读与译记：

子曰：“《关雎》乐而不淫，哀而不伤。”（《论语》）经孔子这么一说，中国传统爱情诗歌就被定下了基调：“乐”与“哀”都要有节制，不能过分。《诗经》的编纂者把它置于开篇的位置，体现了儒家的婚恋观——恋爱要以结婚、建立家庭为最终目的。儒家认为，用婚姻为纽带来组建家庭，以家庭作为社会的基本单元；家庭和谐和稳定了，整个社会才能安定繁荣。儒家这一传统理念至今还有着积极的传承和借鉴意义。如果，男女双方粘在一起，成天嘴边挂着“三字经”（我爱你），一旦进了婚姻殿堂，双方稍有矛盾，却随时要求分手，类似过家家，那社会岂能融洽、安定？

《关雎》里面的“君子”想追求一位“淑女”的心理活动，被刻画得既真切又传神。“关关雎鸠，在河之洲”这两句是“兴”，用鸟儿聚在一起，鸣叫求友的场面，引发读者的联想，从而过渡到青年男女的求爱上。“兴”这一创作手法，在中国古典诗词里非常常见。又如在《诗经·小雅》的《伐木》里，“嘤其鸣矣，求其友声”，鸟儿之间的和鸣，不仅是求友之声，也是求偶的叫唤。译文中添增 seeking company，更能凸显前面的“关关”之声，体现它也是为了求友、求爱。用这样的方法处理，不会让英文读者觉得突兀，或文气不够连贯。在译文的第三行开头，增加了 behold 一词，起到了过渡作用，使下文的“窈窕淑女，君子好逑”，很自然地跟男女之间的爱情活动紧密联系在一起了。

诗中“左右流之”里的“流”，意思是“求”“索取”，此处意为“采摘”，与水流无涉。“左右”有千方百计、想方设法之意，因此，这里译为 by all means。采摘荇菜是如此，追求可心的女孩子也一样，既要认真对待，又要心态平和而有分寸。“左右”反复出现，体现了《关雎》这样民歌色彩很鲜明的诗歌的特色——一唱三叹。

君子于役

选自先秦《诗经·王风》

君子于役，
不知其期，
曷至哉？
鸡栖于埘[1]，
日之夕矣，
羊牛下来。
君子于役，
如之何勿思？

君子于役，

My Husband Is Far Away in Service

Selected from *Wangfeng*, *The Book of Songs* in the Pre-Qin Period

My husband is far away in service;
I wonder how long the service term is.
When shall he come back home?
The chickens for roost are home
When the sun is hanging low in the west;
The sheep and cattle are downhill for rest.
My husband is far away in service,
How can I not help missing him?

My husband is far away in service;

不日不月，

曷其有佸[2]？

鸡栖于桀，

日之夕矣，

羊牛下括[3]。

君子于役，

苟[4]无饥渴？

I wonder how long his serivce term is.

When could we have a family reunion?

The chickens are homeward for the pen;

The sun is setting low in the west;

The sheep and cattle are back for rest.

My husband is far away in service;

Could he be free from hunger and thirst?

注释：

①埘：筑在墙洞里的鸡窝。

②曷其有佸：何时家庭能团聚。曷，何时。佸，相聚。

③括：通“佸”，此指放牧回来，把牛羊关在一起。

④苟：意为“大概”“也许”，表示猜想。

解读与译记：

丈夫去边远的地方服役了，一去经年，妻子孤零零地待在家中。妻子形单影只，过着寂寞凄凉的日子。白天有自己的劳作，对丈夫的思念可以暂时放在一边，可一到夕阳西下，夜之将临，看看人家的夫君从地里干活回家了，连鸡鸭牛羊等家禽家畜都纷纷归来了，唯独不见她丈夫的身影。这是何等失落和凄凉，真是“教我如何不想他”。这就是最早记录妻子思念丈夫的哀愁的相思民歌《君子于役》。

诗里的“君子”，从他有义务去边远地方服役，又要受饥渴之折磨来推断，社会地位并不会很高。与在嗣后的封建社会里，妻子称丈夫为“官人”同理，这里译作 my husband。

第二节里的“不日不月”应该理解为“日复一日，不知归期”，跟“白天”“晚上”毫无关系。因此这里就译作I wonder how long his serivce term is，跟第一节的“不知其期”是一个意思。民歌体的诗歌，多用重叠的章句，用以渲染情感和气氛，同时也使诗歌更具整体性、节奏感和韵律美。

蒹　葭

选自先秦《诗经·秦风》

蒹葭①苍苍，
白露为霜。
所谓伊人②，
在水一方。
溯洄③从之，
道阻且长。
溯游从之，
宛在水中央。

蒹葭萋萋，

The Reeds

Selected from *Qinfeng*, *The Book of Songs* in the Pre-Qin Period

On the river banks the reeds virescent

Are coated with autumn dew-frost.

Where on earth is my sweet-heart?

She is on the river bank opposite.

I'll go upstream to look for her,

The road is long and also difficult.

I'll go downstream to look for her,

It seems as if she's in the middle of water.

On the river banks the reeds luxuriant

白露未晞[4]。

所谓伊人，

在水之湄[5]。

溯洄从之，

道阻且跻[6]。

溯游从之，

宛在水中坻[7]。

蒹葭采采，

白露未已。

所谓伊人，

在水之涘[8]。

溯洄从之，

道阻且右[9]。

溯游从之，

宛在水中沚[10]。

Are still bedewed early in the morn.
Where on earth is my sweet-heart?
She's just on the other river margin.
I'll go upstream to look for her,
But the steep road is hard to scale.
I'll go downstream to look for her,
It seems as if she's on the river isle.

On the river banks the reeds verdant
Remain dewy in the morn bright.
Where on earth is my dear?
She's at the other end of the river.
I'll go upstream to look for her,
But the road is rough and tortuous.
I'll go downstream to look for her,
It seems as if she's on the islet in the river.

注释：

①蒹葭：芦苇。

②伊人：那个人，指思慕的意中人。

③溯洄：逆河流上行。下面的“溯游”，就是顺流下行。从上下文判断，这里的上行和下行都是沿河步行。

④晞：晒干。

⑤湄：岸边。

⑥跻：升高。

⑦坻：水中高出的小块陆地。

⑧涘：水边。

⑨右：迂回曲折。

⑩沚：水中小沙洲。

解读与译记：

这首《蒹葭》由三个诗节组成，每一节的开头，都描写芦苇上的浓霜随着太阳光的照射而变化，以此来衬托诗人感情的变化起伏。第一节写芦苇“白露为霜”(Are coated with autumn dew-frost)，意思是也许此时太阳还未升起，深秋的霜露浓重地结在苇叶上。诗人触景生情，忽然想到他的意中人，她很有可能在河的对面吧。他想不顾一切地去找她呀：逆流而上，翻山越岭，不顾道路崎岖去寻找，但她还是杳无踪影；顺流而下去寻吧，也许她会在某个水域中出现了。第二节里，太阳升起，芦苇上的浓霜还是没有融化，“白露未晞”(Are still bedewed early in the morning)，他还想不畏艰险去找她，这时她又仿佛出现在水中的一块滩头上。第三节里，可能太阳已经升得很高了，可是“白露未已”(Remain dewy in the morn bright)，他还不愿放弃追寻，顺水、逆流去寻找，却依稀觉得他的意中人正亭亭玉立，出现在远处的水中沙洲上……他(当事人)不离不弃，苦苦追寻，到头来还是一无所获。仿佛被追寻的美人仅仅是水中月、镜中花，始终是一个可望而不可即的幻影！这种浪漫主义的手法，更易让读者被当事人所感动，钦佩他对爱情的那份专注和执着。即便是现在的读者，也不可能不为所动吧？

为了体现“整体中有变化”，像“苍苍”“萋萋”“采采”几乎都是“茂盛”的意思，但笔者分别用virescent，luxuriant和verdant来翻译。

以上三首诗，都选自《诗经》。入选我国这部最早的诗歌总集的作品，原先大多是在民间以口头形式流传，后来经过文人加工整理，形成固定文字版本。因此这些诗篇的民歌特色非常明显。比如，经常采用比兴的手法，特别是“兴”，更为常见。而“反复”，又是另一大特点。在一唱三叹的反复中，去加强它的诗意和节奏感，也使得诗歌更具连贯性和整体性。同时，这种反复，也不是机械的重复，而是每次都将一些字词做了改变和调整，既避免枯燥，又具有更多内涵。在翻译时，要注意相应做到“整体中有变化”。变化，是为了文字更为生动。

上　邪

汉乐府民歌

上邪[1]！我欲与君相知[2]，长命无绝衰。山无陵，江水为竭，冬雷震震，夏雨[3]雪，天地合[4]，乃敢与君绝[5]！

Heaven Above

A Yuefu Ballad in the Han Dynasties

Heaven above! I vow to love you for ever and ever. I would never give you up until mountains collapse, rivers go dry, thunder rolls in winter, snow flies in summer, heaven falls and earth subsides!

注释：

①上邪：天哪！

②相知：称为知己。

③雨：此处为动词，意为“下”（雪）。

④天地合：天与地合二为一。

⑤绝：断了（恋爱）关系。

解读与译记：

这首民歌以一个追求爱情的少女的口吻对天发誓，要永远爱她的意中人，只有出现山崩地裂、江河枯竭、冬雷滚滚、夏日降雪等不太可能出现的情况时才敢“与君绝”，充分表达了她对爱情的忠贞不贰。如此直接、热烈和执着地向对方表达爱意，在文人诗词里是很少见的。这样不管不顾的求爱方式，更显出这女孩的真诚和决心，也使这位心口如一、快人快语的姑娘的形象跃然纸上。

“上邪”是对天发誓的“呼告”，类似“苍天在上”“老天做证”或“对天发誓”（Heaven above）。“长命无绝衰”译作 for ever and ever,是否有点“此爱绵绵无绝期”的意思呢?“山无陵”可以理解为“山垮塌成了土丘”,因此译作mountains collapse。

用发誓的形式来表达对爱情矢志不渝,在域外诗歌里也不乏例子。比如,苏格兰诗人彭斯在《一朵红红的玫瑰》里唱道:“即便大海干涸断了水,/太阳把岩石化为灰烬;/我会更加爱你,我的宝贝,/只要我还有一息生命。”(Till a' the seas gang dry, my dear, / And the rocks melt wi' the sun; / O I will luve thee still, my dear, / While the sands o' life shall run.)

行行重行行

选自汉《古诗十九首》

行行重行行，

与君生别离。

相去万余里，

各在天一涯[1]。

道路阻[2]且长，

会面安可知！

胡马[3]依北风，

越鸟[4]巢南枝。

相去日已远，

衣带日已缓[5]。

Keep Going from Me

Selected from *Nineteen Ancient Poems* in the Han Dynasties

Going, keeping going, you are going away from me,

Leaving me all alone far away from thee.

As a result, we two are far apart separated;

I'm here while you're at the earth's other end.

The journey there is long and difficult;

I wonder when we shall again each other meet.

The north-born horse coming south likes to face wind north;

The south-bred bird going north tends to nestle on branches south.

The longer the time of our separation is,

The looser my girdle for my waist becomes.

浮云蔽白日，

游子不顾反。

思君令人老，

岁月忽已晚。

弃捐[6]勿复道，

努力加餐饭。

The floating clouds tend to hide the light of the sun;

Travelling out long, you seem unwilling to home return.

For missing you too much, I'm pining away day by day;

And very soon this year is seen passing away.

I have no more complaint of your negligence of me;

Taking care of yourself is what I'd like to say to thee.

注释：

①天一涯：天各一方。

②阻：崎岖。

③胡马：在北方长大的马。

④越鸟：南方所产的鸟。

⑤缓：宽松。

⑥弃捐：抛开，(被)抛弃。下面接着两句的意思是：我也不再说抱怨的话了，虽有万语千言，归结成一句话，那就是：你要多多珍惜身体(加餐饭)。

解读与译记：

这首《行行重行行》是《古诗十九首》中的首篇，大约是东汉末年的作品；它表达了一位妇女因丈夫出门远行，迟迟不归而产生的深深思念之情。

丈夫可能是外出谋生，不惜离开，让年轻的妻子独守空闺。作为他的妻子，当然会产生思念、生发离愁，甚至嗔怪丈夫一去之后，音信杳然。

“行行重行行”，用白话来表达，就是“走呀走，不停地走着”,似乎难以有尽头。古代交通不便,出行多为徒步,靠着一双脚,一步步地走,像丈量土地般地挨到目的地。山高路远、乘船过坝自不待言,途中遇到虎豹豺狼或强人土匪也很有可能。这怎能不使独自留守家中的妻子牵肠挂肚呢? 所以,“道路阻且长,会面安可知”这样的担心,在她心中难以抹去。思之愈深,愁之愈切! 由于担心和思念过度,“相去日已远,衣带日已缓”,真是“思君令人老”。在万般无奈中,她也埋怨过,甚至出现一种猜疑心理——“浮云蔽白日,游子不顾反”。到底丈夫是由于活计的拖累不能速速还家,还是另有什么缘由呢? 然而,嗔怪归嗔怪,她最终还是希望丈夫要多多珍重,以期早日平安归来,夫妻团聚。整首诗充满矛盾心理,使一个立体的思妇形象跃然纸上,让读者过目难忘。

诗中“胡马依北风,越鸟巢南枝”两行对仗,可以看作“兴”语,用自然现象表现对丈夫的埋怨:动物都知道依恋故土,何况人乎? 翻译时,如果不影响意思的表达,尽可能在对仗这一形式上有所体现。这里译作 The north-born horse coming south likes to face wind north; / The south-bred bird going north tends to nestle on branches south,是否多少可以看出点对仗的味道来了呢?“衣带日已缓”即“衣带渐宽”之意,这里译作 The looser my girdle for my waist becomes。“思君令人老”中的“老”不译作 age,而译成 pining away day by day,因为这里的“老”跟“为伊消得人憔悴”中“憔悴”的意思相仿。

杂　诗(其四)

〔三国魏〕曹　植

南国①有佳人，

容华②若桃李。

朝游江北岸，

夕宿潇湘沚③。

时俗薄朱颜④，

谁为发皓齿⑤？

俯仰⑥岁将暮，

荣耀⑦难久恃⑧。

Miscellaneous Poem (Ⅳ)

By Cao Zhi (Wei Kingdom of the Three Kingdoms Period)

In the southern land lives a dazzling beauty
Whose aspect is as peach flowers as pretty.
She tours on the north bank in the morn,
And puts up on the Xiang Isle in the even.
Social customs scorn the woman pretty;
Who'd like to recommend her to society?
Almost in a wink one would old become;
The glory of beauty would last seldom.

众里寻他千百度

注释:

①南国:泛指江南一带。

②容华:容貌。

③湘沚:湘水中的小洲。沚,指水中小洲。朝游北岸,夕宿湘沚,以湘水女神自喻,取自屈原《九歌》。此句一作“日夕宿湘沚”。

④薄朱颜:不重视貌美如花的人。这里暗指不重视有才德的人。

⑤发皓齿:这里指推荐、介绍。

⑥俯仰:低头扬头之间,言时间之短暂。

⑦荣耀:青春盛颜。

⑧久恃:久留,久待。

解读与译记:

屈原常以香草美人自喻(如《离骚》之“惟草木之零落兮,恐美人之迟暮”),曹植这首诗也像是从《离骚》中脱胎而出的。自屈原以后,凡自认为“才高八斗”却又抱负难展的读书人,差不多都会自喻为“香草美人”。这首诗,看起来是写一位绝色美人

"朝游江北岸，夕宿潇湘沚"（来无影，去无踪），但又受到世俗的摈弃和不屑，甚至嫉妒。根据一直以来诗家的确认，这的确是一首以"香草美人"自喻的寄托之作。牢骚之语"时俗薄朱颜，谁为发皓齿？"也许正是曹植为曹丕、曹叡所打压，在发泄愤愤不平的情绪吧。

笔者觉得，把它归于"有所它指"的寄托之作，实在有些煞风景，还不如实实在在将其看作一首仰慕和颂扬美女的爱情诗更好。所以，笔者在翻译时，是完全把它当作爱情诗来处理的。像安德鲁·马维尔（Andrew Marvell）《赠给他的羞怯女友》（*To His Coy Mistress*）那样直接地去赞美心爱的女友有多好："我要花一百年时间来赞美 / 你的双眸，欣赏你的蛾眉； / 要用两百年膜拜你的酥胸， / 赞遍你周身得花三万个秋冬。"（A hundred years should go to praise / Thine eyes, and on thy forhead gaze; / Two hundred to adore each breast, / But thirty thousand to the rest.）

"俯仰岁将暮"中"俯仰"意为"转瞬即逝"。"岁"为年华。整句意思是"转瞬之间年华老去"。

闺怨篇

〔南朝陈〕江　总

寂寂青楼①大道边，
纷纷白雪绮窗②前。
池上鸳鸯不独自，
帐中苏合③还空然④。
屏风有意障明月，
灯火无情照独眠。
辽西⑤水冻春应少，
蓟北鸿来路几千。
愿君关山及早度，
念妾桃李⑥片时妍⑦。

Chamber Lament

By Jiang Zong (Chen Kingdom of the Southern and Northern Dynasties)

By the road a lonely green mansion's standing;
Outside the lattice window a snow's flurrying.
Mandarin ducks never paddle singly in the pool;
Behind the curtain storax is burning to no avail.
The screen shades the moonlight as if purposely;
While the lamp flares coldly on the awake one lonely.
Spring in Liaoxi frontier is short with frozen rivers;
Letters from Jibei fortress'd travel thousands of miles.
How I wish my husband returned earlier despite of distance!
For my prime of youth and beauty'd soon vanish without trace.

注释：

①青楼：刷成青色的楼房。

②绮窗：雕花的格子窗。

③苏合：苏合香，一种香草制成的香料，可以入药；另一说是几种香草混合制成的香料。

④然：同“燃”。

⑤辽西：与下文的“蓟北”皆为地名，都在今河北境内。这里指的是边防和战略要地。

⑥桃李：如花的青春年华。

⑦妍：盛开。

解读与译记：

自《诗经》伊始，像反映“君子从远役，佳人守茕独”这样的“闺怨”之作，可说是层见叠出。这首《闺怨篇》，只是为数众多抒发闺阁怨情的诗章中的一篇。诗中描述一位丈夫从远役的深闺佳人，在一个初雪飘落的日子，因寒气袭人，独守空闺，彻夜难眠。虽然家中条件优越，闺房里华贵家具几乎一应俱全：

彩绘的屏风，映照着暖暖的红烛之光；扑鼻的苏合香，充满了整个温馨的闺房……这样的氛围，本应该跟丈夫共享，可是“万事俱备只欠东风”，其另一半却在戍边呢！她现在守着偌大的一座楼房，更觉寂寞难耐。更为恼人的是，他们的住宅紧靠着大路，那络绎不绝，为各自生活奔忙着的人们，也许正顶着风雪往家里赶，去享受各自家庭的天伦之乐。因为对丈夫的念念不忘，她想到了池水中成双成对的鸳鸯，它们是多幸福和自在呀！而我呢，丈夫在千里之外的边防线上经受着严寒的考验，即便是一封书信，往来也得有几千里路的驿程。夫君啊，你能否早早归来跟我团聚呀，我的青春在思念中消磨，只怕相见之时，我早已朱颜难再了！

此诗写于南朝陈，作品体现当时雕琢字句的风气，多用排偶，描写入微。十个诗句，五双对偶，在翻译中，很难表现这个形式。只有在一、二及七、八等句的译文中，译者能隐约透露点这方面的意图。

在前八句诗中，初看未见思妇的情感流露，但诗人还是很巧妙地将她的寂寞相思、愁肠百结的心态渗透在字里行间，比如“寂寂”(lonely)、“独自”(singly)、“空然”(burning to no avail)、“有意”(purposely)、“独眠”(awake one lonely)等。这就是我国传统诗词表达的高明之处：把浓烈的情感包裹起来，伺机待发，或者将其悄然融于意象之中。

寄阮郎[1]

〔隋〕张碧兰

郎如洛阳花[2]，
妾似武昌柳[3]。
两地惜春风，
何时一携手？

To My Lover

By Zhang Bilan（the Sui Dynasty）

You， my lover， are like a peony in Luoyang

And me， your love， a willow in Wuchang.

In two places though， spring is the same cherished;

Yet when could we get together hand in hand?

注释：

①阮郎：是一个人物典故，指成仙而去的人或情郎。阮郎的原型人物是汉代的阮肇。后诗文中常用“刘郎”“阮郎”“刘阮”“阮刘”“阮肇”等指情郎，亦指成仙而去的人。

②洛阳花：一说是石竹的别称。洛阳以盛产牡丹闻名，故笔者认为译作牡丹花更合适。

③武昌柳：自晋代陶侃在武昌种柳后，“武昌柳”在诗歌中就泛指柳树。

解读与译记：

这是一首仅有二十字的短小情诗。主人公是位风华正茂的青年女性，她爱恋着一位风度翩翩的小伙。但是他们俩却偏偏两地暌隔，想见上一面也很不易。怎么办呢？只能用诗来表达自己的情愫。

我的情郎啊，在我心中你似一朵洛阳的牡丹花，是那么华贵俊秀、气度不凡；而我呢，也并非配不上你的泛泛之辈呀：我似“碧玉妆成一树高，万条垂下绿丝绦”的柳树，迎风摆舞、婀娜多姿。我们虽身处两地，但同样珍惜浪漫的春天，“两地惜春风”呀。这句诗是全诗最为关键的表述，它的深层意思是：我俩都知道青春短暂、转瞬即逝，既然彼此相爱，就该早早走在一起。在最后一句里，以疑问句的形式来表达“我们为何不早日牵手共修百年之好”的迫切心愿。

“两地惜春风”(In two places though, spring is the same cherished)，妙语双关：从时令上说，写诗的时候正值万物更新的春天；深层的意思是，我俩都处于青春年华，要分外珍惜这千金难买的人生花季，为何不早早结成连理呀！译文中增加though和the same就使得内涵表达更为明确。

闺　怨

〔唐〕王昌龄

闺中少妇不曾愁，
春日凝妆[1]上翠楼[2]。
忽见陌头[3]杨柳色，
悔教夫婿觅封侯[4]。

Chamber Lament

By Wang Changling (the Tang Dynasty)

The young lady in the chamber is always free from care;
On a spring day she climbs the tower with fully-set hair.
The moment she sees the green willows in the fields vast,
She begins to regret urging her husband to seek a royal post.

注释：

①凝妆：打扮得很隆重。

②翠楼：大户人家院子里的楼阁，一般要高出院内其他房子。

③陌头：田野。

④封侯：册封到爵位。这里统指封官加爵，做上高官。

解读与译记：

这又是一曲闺中少妇思夫的哀歌。

第一句有的版本作“闺中少妇不知愁”；“不知”不像“不曾”那样，没有一种先后对照的意思。本来丈夫外出谋取功名，妻子独守空闺倒也没有什么，可是自己今日打扮得漂漂亮亮，登上了楼阁，放眼望去春色恼人：阡陌之间柳绿桃红，寻春踏青的人络绎不绝——有举家寻春的，有对对情侣手牵着手出游的……见到这一切，自己再也无心览赏春色了，一股子悔意袭上心头，真的太后悔当初鼓励乃至怂恿自己的丈夫去谋取功名、跻身仕途了！

“闺中少妇不曾愁”译作 The young lady in the chamber is

always free from care，突出她总是那么无忧无虑，因为嫁入了富人之家，衣食无忧，哪曾尝到愁的滋味呢？但这也为后面心理的突然变化埋下伏笔。后来情感的急剧扭转，体现在“忽见”(the moment)、“悔教”(begins to regret)上面，也就显得水到渠成了。

题都城南庄

〔唐〕崔　护

去年今日此门中，

人面桃花相映红。

人面只今何处去，

桃花依旧笑春风。

Written on the Wall of a Village House South of the Capital

By Cui Hu (the Tang Dynasty)

This day of last year, in this gate of the house, I got a glimpse of a beauty,
Whose charming face was as attractive as pink peach blossoms.

Alas! Whoever could tell me today where I could find the beauty?

The spring wind says "No!", smiling as ever with peach blossoms blooming.

解读与译记：

根据唐代孟启《本事诗》可知，这首诗的背后确有一段颇具传奇色彩的故事。这是诗人的一次亲身经历，也可以说是一次抱恨终身的“艳遇”。诗人在清明节那天去郊外踏青，大约来之前饮酒过量，到了都城南郊，酒劲发作，口渴难耐，于是走到花木掩映的一户人家门口，想讨一碗水喝。只见大门紧闭，寂寂无人，他便敲开了门。应门的是一位妙龄女郎，她落落大方地拿来水给他喝。在这空隙，诗人只见那少女倚着院子里一株盛开的桃树伫立，真可谓“人面桃花相映红”！那女子并不开口说什么，只是默默望着他。诗人倍感惶惑，不知所措地匆匆离去，竟然连感谢的话也不曾说。可以想见，这以后的三百六十五日，诗人时不时会在眼前重现当时的情景。于是，第二年的清明节终于到来时，怀着满腔的希望，诗人想继续他们前一年的“故事”。可谁知来到这宅门，只见大门紧锁；四顾无人，竟无法得知这户人家的下落。当然，这美女嘛，也像《聊斋》里的狐仙，杳无踪迹了。从偶遇佳人，继而念念不忘，到次年再次寻访未果，其懊丧失落的情绪只用区区二十八个字便描画得如此荡气回肠，得到几多读者的共鸣和追捧！

“人面只今何处去”，在有的版本中作“人面不知何处去”。笔者觉得，“只今”比“不知”更能体现诗人那种怅然若失的慨叹；“不知”仅仅是客观的叙述，而“只今”有“可是今天呢”之意，更能体现诗人懊丧的情绪。“桃花依旧笑春风”，物是人非，情何以堪？这最后一句译作 The spring wind says “No!”, smiling as ever with peach blossoms blooming。春风无情，断然说道，“一无所知”，还幸灾乐祸地跟桃花一起讪笑着呢！这真是：虽然人有爱意，怎奈“春色无情”啊！

长恨歌

〔唐〕白居易

汉皇[1]重色[2]思倾国[3]，
御宇[4]多年求不得。
杨家有女[5]初长成，
养在深闺人未识。
天生丽质难自弃，
一朝选在君王侧。
回眸一笑百媚生，
六宫粉黛[6]无颜色[7]。
春寒赐浴华清池[8]，
温泉水滑洗凝脂[9]。

Song of Endless Lament

By Bai Juyi (the Tang Dynasty)

As an amorous man, the Emperor's longing for a stunning beauty;

Yet for years, he had sought in vain within his sovereignty.

A maiden born to the Yang's had just come to womanhood,

Bred deep in the chamber, never known to people outside.

Endowed with peerless beauty by nature hard to be concealed,

She was one day summoned to serve at the Emperor's own side.

Turning with a smile, she fascinated so many beholders with charm

That the fully-arrayed concubines were overshadowed in the harem.

In chilly spring she was bestowed a bath in the Huaqing Imperial Pool;

In its warm spring, her skin soft and glossy seemed just like solidified butter.

侍儿[10]扶起娇无力，
始是新承恩泽[11]时。
云鬟[12]花颜金步摇[13]，
芙蓉帐[14]暖度春宵。
春宵[15]苦短日高起，
从此君王不早朝。
承欢侍宴无闲暇，
春从春游夜专夜。
后宫佳丽三千[16]人，
三千宠爱在一身。
金屋[17]妆成娇侍夜，
玉楼宴罢醉和春。
姐妹弟兄皆列土[18]，
可怜[19]光彩生门户。
遂令天下父母心，

So delicate after bath, she should have attendants support her;

For it's the first time that she'd begun to bask in His Majesty's own favor.

With gold hairpins on cloud-like dark hair she looked so sweet

That His Majesty spent the first night with her in their love nest.

Nights with his love seemed too short to get up early in the morn,

So that he'd grudged going to daily cabinet meetings since then.

Favored by the Emperor, she'd always stay at his side drinking with him;

Spring after spring, they seemed inseparable at play or in the bedroom.

Though many a concubine in the harem was as beautiful as a goddess,

Never moved by their beauty, His Majesty pinned on her the love of his.

Fully-set in "the golden house", she was made ready to sleep with the Emperor;

After feasts in a gorgeous banquet-hall, they'd often go to bed drunk together.

Her sisters and brothers were all conferred on fertile land without any feats;

Noble members of the Yang family became the envy of the common people.

Then, fathers and mothers in the empire chose to have this same ideal

不重生男重生女。

骊宫[20]高处入青云，

仙乐风飘处处闻。

缓歌慢舞凝丝竹[21]，

尽日君王看不足。

渔阳[22]鼙鼓[23]动地来，

惊破霓裳羽衣曲[24]。

九重城阙[25]烟尘生[26]，

千乘万骑西南行。[27]

翠华摇摇行复止，

西出都门百余里。[28]

六军[29]不发无奈何，

宛转[30]蛾眉[31]马前死。

花钿[32]委地[33]无人收，

翠翘金雀玉搔头。[34]

That they didn't wish to give birth to a baby boy rather than a little girl.
Grand Huaqing Palace towering to clouds on the north slope of Lishan
Was sending melodious music with the wind to all sides and everyone.
Songs and dances were fully in tune, with orchestral music, entirely vivid;
His Majesty was watching performances daily, his desire never subdued.
Unexpectedly, came the sounds of war-drums, making such a disturbance
That the tune of *Rainbow Skirt and Feather Garment* reduced to silence.
The walls and towers in the Imperial Palace were permeated in war clouds;
Much scared, His Majesty began to flee southwest protected by his guards.
Imperial Guards with flowery dragon flags fluttering stopped now and then;
One hundred miles west of the capital, their group arrived at Mawei Post.
Disobedient, the Imperial Guards beyond all reason refused to go any farther;
Feeling aggrieved, the sentimental beauty had to commit suicide under pressure.
Her jade hairpins like golden birds with kingfisher wings were riches rarely found,
And what a pity, they were heedlessly scattered here and there all over the ground.

君王掩面救不得，

回看血泪相和流。

黄埃散漫风萧索，

云栈[35]萦纡登剑阁[36]。

峨嵋山[37]下少人行，

旌旗无光日色薄。

蜀江水碧蜀山青，

圣主朝朝暮暮情。

行宫[38]见月伤心色，

夜雨闻铃[39]肠断声。

天旋地转[40]回龙驭[41]，

到此踌躇不能去。

马嵬坡下泥土中，

不见玉颜[42]空死处。

君臣相顾尽沾衣，

Unable to save his sweet-heart, the Emperor was almost drowned in tears,
Turning about, he got a glimpse of the sad scene with blood and tears.
The bleak autumn wind mixed with yellow dust was scattering dead leaves;
The winding plank road on cliffs led the royal troops to the Jianmen Pass.
Steep and narrow, the Shu trails in Mount Emei saw travelers seldom;
It's drawing toward sunset, and fainter and fainter, flags and banners all'd seem.
The torrential waters of Shu were blue and its towering mountains were green;
His Majesty was sad at her death and he thought of their former affections very often.
At the moon in the palace the Emperor was filled with sorrow quite often;
At the ring of the bell during a rainy night, he'd soon feel heart-broken.
With the turmoil of war settled the Emperor's carriage started to go home;
At Mawei Post, His Majesty came to a standstill trying to find his honey's tomb.
In the desolate dust at Mawei Post where her grave once was,

The matchless beauty was no longer seen leaving the place in green grass.
His Majesty and the imperial officials all looked at one another in tears;

东望都门信马[43]归。

归来池苑皆依旧，

太液[44]芙蓉未央柳。

芙蓉如面柳如眉，

对此如何不泪垂？

春风桃李花开日，

秋雨梧桐叶落时。

西宫南内[45]多秋草，

落叶满阶红不扫。

梨园弟子[46]白发新，

椒房[47]阿监[48]青娥[49]老。

夕殿萤飞思悄然，

孤灯挑尽[50]未成眠。

迟迟[51]钟鼓初长夜，

耿耿[52]星河欲曙天[53]。

Looking east to the capital's gate they were riding giving free rein to their horses.
Back to Chang'an they found that gardens and lotus pools remained as before.
So were both lotus flowers in Taiye Pool and willows in Weiyang Palace.
Lotus flowers seemed like her face and willows' leaves seemed like her brows,
And everything there reminded them of the dead beauty, making everyone burst into tears.
Pear and peach blossoms in spring as ever, yet sadly the beauty was nowhere to be seen;
The autumn rain pattering on phoenix trees made one feel all the more sad and heart-broken.
Rank autumnal grass ran wild everywhere in the West Hall and the South Palace;
Dead red leaves scattering over the stairs were no longer swept by anyone in the palace.
Operatic players nice and young then were growing old with grey hair
And for the concubines in the harems, had been long past their prime and luster.
Seeing the fireflies in the palace at night, His Majesty couldn't but think of her;
Without a wink of sleep all night, he often raised the wick to make brighter.
The more he counted the tolls of drum and bell, the longer he felt the night;
With the stars fading and light growing, he kept fully awake all night.

鸳鸯瓦[54]冷霜华[55]重，
翡翠衾[56]寒谁与共[57]。
悠悠生死别经年，
魂魄不曾来入梦。
临邛道士鸿都客，[58]
能以精诚致魂魄[59]。
为感君王辗转思，
遂教方士[60]殷勤[61]觅。
排空驭气[62]奔如电，
升天入地求之遍。
上穷[63]碧落[64]下黄泉[65]，
两处茫茫皆不见。
忽闻海上有仙山[66]，
山在虚无缥缈间。
楼阁玲珑[67]五云[68]起，

The tiles like birds of love were coated in thick layers with cold hoar-frost;

The green silk quilt was chilly to the skin, so whoever could with him share it?

The separation between the lovebirds in life and death had lasted years long;

Nowhere found, the soul of his honey had never come to his dreams all along.

There was in Sichuan a well-known Taoist, who happened to stay in the capital;

It's said that he could, with magic arts, call back the dead one's soul.

The Emperor was thinking of his love, tossing about and pining from day to day,

So necromancers were sent to look for her, carefully and thoroughly every day.

Some searchers were going like riding clouds in the sky, or rushing about like lightening;

They'd searched everywhere up in heaven or down to earth, finding nothing.

They'd looked for her everywhere either in the vast heaven or all in the underworld,

In the ample cloudy sky and on the boundless land not a single soul had been found.

Suddenly came the news that there was a fairy mount named Penglai on the East Sea,

The peak of which poking to the sky seemed faint in dense clouds and in smoke misty.

Exquisitely built, the towers and pavilions were surrounded by clouds colorful,

其中绰约[69]多仙子。

中有一人字太真，

雪肤花貌参差[70]是。

金阙[71]西厢叩玉扃[72]，

转教小玉报双成。[73]

闻道汉家天子使，

九华帐[74]里梦魂惊。

揽衣推枕起徘徊，

珠箔银屏[75]迤逦[76]开。

云鬓半偏新睡觉[77]，

花冠不整下堂来。

风吹仙袂[78]飘飘举，

犹似霓裳羽衣舞。

玉容寂寞[79]泪阑干[80]，

梨花一枝春带雨。

In which there were a lot of goddesses and fairies, statuesque and graceful.

Among the thousands of beautiful fairies there was one by the name of Taizhen;

With snow-white skin she was pretty as a flower, who looked like the very person.

So the Taoist went to the west Golden Hall and knocked at the jasper door;

And asked the maid to make another maidservant report the arrival of the envoy.

The moment she got the news that the Emperor's envoy was just at the door,

Fairy Taizhen was startled out of her sweet dreams in her flowered canopy.

Pushing her pillow aside and putting on her coat, she got up in a hurry pacing around;

Pearl curtains and silver screens were opened one after another around the room.

She'd just waked up, for her hair was loose and undone, hiding half the face of hers;

Disregarding that her hair was not properly done, and in a hurry she went downstairs.

The gentle breeze was brushing her ample sleeves, and her steps were light with fairy grace,

As if she were dancing to the tune of *Rainbow Skirt and Feather Garment* in the then palace.

Her features were worried and lonesome, with tears trickling across her cheeks so that

She looked truly like a branch of pear-blossom with rain-drops after a spring shower.

含情凝睇[81]谢君王，
一别音容两渺茫。
昭阳殿[82]里恩爱绝，
蓬莱宫[83]中日月长。
回头下望人寰[84]处，
不见长安见尘雾。
惟将旧物[85]表深情，
钿合金钗寄将去[86]。
钗留一股合一扇，
钗擘黄金合分钿。[87]
但教心似金钿坚，
天上人间会相见。
临别殷勤重寄词[88]，
词中有誓两心知[89]。
七月七日长生殿[90]，

Gazing tenderly on the envoy, she entrusted him with gratitude for the Emperor,
For they'd never been heard of nor seen each other for long since their departure.
The abiding affectionate relation at the Zhaoyang Palace had been broken off
And at the Penglai Hall she'd been living endlessly a fairy life.

Turning around and looking down at the earthly world in which people reside,
She didn't see the capital Chang'an but the thick and vast expanse of fog instead.
To express her deep love for the Emperor, she sent him some keepsakes old,
Such as gold hairpins with gold-foiled boxes, trying to do whatever now she could.
She kept half of both her hairpins and gold-foiled boxes, the other half for him, her dear,
And they each would keep these tokens as their own personal treasures for ever.
She wished that their two hearts were like these keepsakes which were firm and solid
And they would someday meet at last either up in the heaven or down in the human world.
At his departure she begged the Taoist to express her deep love for the Emperor;
Whatever word sent to the Emperor could only be known by themselves together.
They had met at the Longevity Hall on the night of the seventh of seventh month that year;

夜半无人私语时。

在天愿作比翼鸟[91]，

在地愿为连理枝[92]。

天长地久有时尽，

此恨[93]绵绵[94]无绝期。

In their whispers at midnight, they two had vowed to heaven their love for each other.

In the heaven, they were willing to fly wing to wing happily like two love birds;

On the earth, they would become two trees interlocked together with branches.

Even though heaven and earth seemed so everlasting and ever endure,

Only their eternal lament of life and death could linger for ever.

注释：

①汉皇：原指汉武帝刘彻。此处借指唐玄宗李隆基。唐人文学创作常以汉称唐。

②重色：爱好女色。

③倾国：绝色女子。汉代李延年对汉武帝唱了一首歌："北方有佳人，绝世而独立。一顾倾人城，再顾倾人国。宁不知倾国与倾城，佳人难再得。"后来，"倾国倾城"就成为美女的代称。

④御宇：驾御宇内，即统治天下。

⑤杨家有女：蜀州司户杨玄琰，有女名杨玉环。她先被册封为玄宗之子寿王李瑁之妃，后被玄宗册封为贵妃。白居易在此谓"养在深闺人未识"，是作者有意为帝王避讳的说法。

⑥六宫粉黛：指宫中所有嫔妃。粉黛本为女性化妆用品，粉以抹脸，黛以描眉，而此处代指六宫中的女性。

⑦无颜色：意为相形之下，都失去了美好的姿容。

⑧华清池：华清池温泉，在今西安市临潼区南的骊山下。唐玄宗每年春季和冬季都到此居住。

⑨凝脂：形容皮肤白嫩滋润，犹如凝固的脂肪。《诗经·卫风·硕人》语"肤如凝脂"。

⑩侍儿：宫女。

⑪新承恩泽：刚得到皇帝的宠幸。

⑫云鬓：源自《木兰诗》之"当窗理云鬓，对镜贴花黄"，形容女子

鬓发盛美如云。

⑬金步摇：一种金首饰，用金银丝盘成花之形状，上面缀着垂珠之类，插于发鬓，走路时摇曳生姿。

⑭芙蓉帐：绣着莲花的帐子。形容帐之精美。

⑮春宵：此处指受皇上临幸的第一晚。

⑯佳丽三千：《后汉书·皇后纪》："自武元之后，世增淫费，乃至掖庭三千。"言后宫女子之多。

⑰金屋：《汉武故事》记载，武帝幼时，他姑妈将他抱在膝上，问他要不要她的女儿阿娇当妻子。他笑着回答说："若得阿娇，当以金屋藏之。"此处指金碧辉煌的后宫。

⑱列土：分封土地。

⑲可怜：可爱，值得羡慕。

⑳骊宫：骊山华清宫。骊山在今陕西西安临潼。

㉑凝丝竹：指弦乐器和管乐器奏出舒缓的旋律。

㉒渔阳：郡名，辖今北京平谷和天津蓟县等地，当时属于平卢、范阳、河东三镇节度史安禄山的辖区。天宝十四载（755），安禄山起兵叛乱，安史之乱爆发。

㉓鼙鼓：骑兵用的小鼓。此处借指安禄山举兵叛唐。

㉔霓裳羽衣曲：舞曲名，乐曲着意表现虚无缥缈的仙境和仙女形象。

㉕九重城阙：指长安。

㉖烟尘生：指发生战事。

㉗千乘万骑西南行：天宝十五载(756)，安禄山破潼关，逼近长安。玄宗带领杨贵妃等出延秋门向西南方向逃走。当时随行护卫并不多，“千乘万骑”是夸大之词。乘：一人一骑为一乘。

㉘“翠华”两句：李隆基西奔至距长安百余里的马嵬驿(今陕西兴平)，扈从禁卫军发难，不再前行，请诛杨国忠、杨玉环兄妹以平民怨。玄宗为保自身，只得照办。

㉙六军：指皇帝的护卫军队。

㉚宛转：形容美人临死前哀怨缠绵的样子。

㉛蛾眉：古代美女的代称，此指杨贵妃。

㉜花钿：用金翠珠宝等制成的花朵形首饰。

㉝委地：丢弃在地上。

㉞翠翘金雀玉搔头：这些都是贵妃的首饰。翠翘，首饰，形如翡翠鸟尾。金雀是金雀钗，钗形似朱雀，故名。玉搔头指玉簪。

㉟云栈萦纡：高入云霄的栈道萦回盘绕。

㊱剑阁：又称剑门关，在今四川剑阁县北，是由秦入蜀的要道。

㊲峨嵋山：峨眉山，在今四川峨眉山市。但玄宗奔蜀途中，并未经过峨眉山。这里泛指蜀中高山。

㊳行宫：皇帝离京出行在外的临时住所。

㊴夜雨闻铃：《明皇杂录·补遗》：“明皇既幸蜀，西南行。初入斜谷，霖雨涉旬，于栈道雨中闻铃音与山相应。上既悼念贵妃，采其声为《雨霖铃曲》以寄恨焉。”

㊵天旋地转：指时局好转。

㊶回龙驭：皇帝的车驾归来。

㊷玉颜：指杨贵妃。

㊸信马：任马前进而不加约制。

㊹太液：汉宫中有太液池。下文的“未央”指汉朝未央宫。两者皆借指唐长安皇宫。

㊺西宫南内：皇宫之内称为大内。西宫即西内太极宫，南内为兴庆宫。玄宗返京后，初居南内。

㊻梨园弟子：指玄宗当年训练的乐工舞女。

㊼椒房：后妃居住之所，因以花椒和泥抹墙，故称。

㊽阿监：宫中的侍从女官。

㊾青娥：年轻的宫女。

㊿孤灯挑尽：古时用油灯照明，为使灯火明亮，过了一会儿就要把浸在油中的灯草往前挑一点。挑尽，表明夜已深。

(51)迟迟：迟缓。报更钟鼓声起止原有定时。这里用以形容玄宗长夜难眠时的心情。

(52)耿耿：微明的样子。

(53)欲曙天：长夜将晓之时。

(54)鸳鸯瓦：屋顶上俯仰相对合在一起的瓦。《三国志·魏书·方技传》载：“文帝梦殿屋两瓦堕地，化为双鸳鸯。”房瓦一俯一仰相合，称阴阳瓦，亦称鸳鸯瓦。

(55)霜华：霜花。

(56)翡翠衾：被单上绣有翡翠鸟的被子。

㊼谁与共：与谁共享。

㊽临邛道士鸿都客：意谓有个从临邛来长安的道士。临邛，今四川邛崃。鸿都，东汉都城洛阳的宫门名，而这里借指长安。

㊾致魂魄：招来杨贵妃的亡魂。

㊿方士：有法术的人。这里指上文中的道士。

61殷勤：尽力。

62排空驭气：腾云驾雾。

63穷：穷尽，找遍。

64碧落：天空。

65黄泉：地下。

66海上有仙山：传说渤海中有蓬莱、方丈、瀛洲三座神山。

67玲珑：华美精巧。

68五云：五彩云霞。

69绰约：体态轻盈柔美。

70参差：仿佛，差不多。

71金阙：上清宫门中有两阙，左金阙，右玉阙。

72玉扃：玉门。

73转教小玉报双成：意为仙府庭院重重，须经辗转通报。小玉、双成皆借指杨贵妃在仙山的侍女。

74九华帐：华丽的帐子。九华，指繁复的花饰图案，形容帐之精美。

75珠箔银屏：珠帘和饰银的屏风。此处极写仙府之华美。

⑯迤逦:接连不断地。

⑰新睡觉:刚睡醒。

⑱袂:衣袖。

⑲寂寞:此指神色黯淡凄楚。

⑳阑干:纵横交错的样子。这里形容泪痕满面。

㉑凝睇:凝视。

㉒昭阳殿:汉成帝宠妃赵飞燕的寝宫。此处借指杨贵妃住过的宫殿。

㉓蓬莱宫:指贵妃在仙山的住处。

㉔人寰:人间。

㉕旧物:指生前与玄宗定情的信物。

㉖寄将去:托道士带回。

㉗"钗留"两句:把金钗、钿盒分成两半,自己留一半。擘,分开。合分钿,将钿盒上的图案分成两部分。

㉘重寄词:贵妃临别时又托道士捎话。

㉙两心知:只有玄宗、贵妃两人心里明白。

㉚长生殿:在骊山华清宫内,是长安皇宫寝殿的习称。

㉛比翼鸟:传说中的鸟名,据说此鸟只有一目一翼,雌雄并在一起才能飞。

㉜连理枝:两株树木树干相抱。古人常用此二物比喻情侣相爱、永不分离。

㉝恨:遗憾。

(94)绵绵：连绵不断。

解读与译记：

《长恨歌》作于806年，是一首叙事和抒情完美结合的长篇叙事诗。它借助唐玄宗、杨贵妃两个历史人物的故事，并根据当时人们的传说，演绎出一首委婉动人、回环曲折的记录爱情悲剧的叙事诗篇。这一诗化的故事，描写的是人们心中常有的那种情感。唐玄宗、杨贵妃这一对历史人物不寻常的恋爱经历和悲惨结局，诗人把其艺术而形象地表现出来，让读者自己去感受、回味这一故事的“恨”，而且是一种“长恨”（“此恨绵绵无绝期”）。

全诗长达一百二十行，大致可分为四个部分。

第一部分，从诗的开头到“尽日君王看不足”。它既揭露唐玄宗的好色，又铺叙杨贵妃“回眸一笑百媚生，六宫粉黛无颜色”的美丽。这一部分讲述了整个悲剧故事的成因：正因为唐玄宗好色，因此他在位的时候便想方设法寻找美艳绝伦的女子来伺候自己，恰巧杨贵妃是一个绝色美人，一得手，唐玄宗哪还有心思管国家的那些“杂事、琐事”呀。于是乎“春宵苦短日高起，从此君王不早朝”。在中国的古代文学作品中，大凡描写改朝换代的历史时，常常出现君王“沉迷女色，祸国殃民”这样的老套情节。果不其然，安史之乱如期而至。

第二部分从“渔阳鼙鼓动地来，惊破霓裳羽衣曲”开始。这一部分写安史之乱爆发，唐玄宗出逃入蜀。当皇帝一行逃到马嵬坡时，御林军发生兵变。护驾的将士们一致逼迫唐玄宗将杨贵妃兄妹处死，否则他们拒绝再往前行。玄宗出于无奈，只得依了将士们，赐死爱妃玉环。爱妃死后，玄宗似被剜去了心头肉，整日闷闷不乐，见月伤心，闻铃落泪；“长恨”也就从此在心头生根。

第三部分从“天旋地转回龙驭”至“魂魄不曾来入梦”。随着叛乱被镇压，玄宗终于回到了京城。然而，皇帝并不为平叛胜利返京露出丝毫欣喜之色，反而因玉环的死去而时时睹物思人，宫廷中任何物件都只能勾起他对爱妃的怀念。日复一日，他夜不成寐，思念之情令其断肠。爱妃一死，阴阳睽违；一晃就几年过去了，可是皇帝成天泣血思念的玉环怎么连梦也未曾托一个给他！

第四部分写的是临邛道士如何用法术招来玉环的亡魂，以解玄宗心头无尽的思念之苦。道士上天入地，终于在海上的蓬莱仙境中找到了一位长相酷似玉环的太真仙子。此人应该就是杨玉环。得知皇帝的使者要找她，她也因为思念玄宗太久而悲喜交加：“玉容寂寞泪阑干，梨花一枝春带雨。”她托使者带信给玄宗，同时还捎去了自己的信物与誓言，回忆在七月七日后半夜的长生殿上，跟心爱的皇上幽会。诗人写了他们的誓言“在天愿作比翼鸟，在地愿为连理枝”，然后带着无尽的感叹“天长地久有时尽，此恨绵绵无绝期”戛然而止，让读者自己猜测、去想象一个结尾。这正是诗人的高明之处。

我国诗歌传统，以抒情诗见长，像《长恨歌》这样长达一百二十行的叙事诗十分少见。

《长恨歌》是以叙事为主调结合抒情来写的。在翻译的时候，就按叙事的惯例，在时态上应该体现故事发展的脉络，以过去时态为主。

这一长篇叙事古诗，其翻译的难点，在于要牵涉许多历史事物（包括古代建筑、器物名称等）和地方的旧有名词。一些当时的器物的名称很难译妥，因为这些旧物，如今很多已经不再存在，而恰恰是这些旧物的名称承载着大量的文化信息，可被称为culture-loaded words。比如“钗留一股合一扇，钗擘黄金合分钿”，这两句的意思是太真把金钗、钿盒分成两半，自留一半，另一半差道士捎给皇上。这里译作She kept half of her hair-pins and gold-foiled boxes, the other half for him, her dear, / And they each would keep these tokens as their own personal treasures for ever，大致意思是：太真将自己贴身的首饰送一半给皇帝当信物，自己留下另一半；希望他能永远当作宝物留在身边，以便睹物思人，不会把她忘掉。“钿合”“金钗”这两个物件在当时是女子闺房梳妆台上不可不备的东西，它们承载着“私密”“珍贵”“体己”等文化信息，要将它们转化为另一种语言，确实难度很大（钿合是什么模样，也许很少有人目睹过）。再如“风吹仙袂飘飖举，犹似霓裳羽衣舞”（The gentle breeze was brushing her ample sleeves, and her steps were light with fairy grace; / As if she were dancing to the tune of *Rainbow Skirt and Feather Garment* in the then palace）中，“仙袂”如果译成 fairy sleeves，就有些滑稽，因此这“仙”气只能跟后面的 grace 合在一起来译。“飘飖举”的内涵也将它分别承载于 ample 和 light 等词语上。“犹似霓裳羽衣舞”这一行表示太真出现时那种轻盈飘逸、道骨仙风的模样，简直好比当年在宫内跳霓裳羽衣舞。译文用了 as if, the then 以及上一行的 fairy grace，来统筹处理。如何总体地表达这两句诗的内涵，要严格守住“意似”。像“渔阳鼙鼓动地来”，说的是安禄山起兵叛乱，战鼓惊天动地，单单译作 Unexpectedly, came the sounds of war-drums, making such a disturbance 就足矣。

对专有名词、文化承载词和古代物件名词的翻译，要做总体权衡：既能突出形象，又承载着文化信息的名词，最好能忠实、细致地译出来，以完整表达原诗的意境；而有些名词很难用译入语传达，就只能译其释义。如果硬要亦步亦趋、依样画葫芦地译出，反而弄巧成拙，使英文读者不知所云、雾里看花。

采莲曲

〔唐〕白居易

菱叶萦波[1]荷飐风[2]，
荷花深处小船通。
逢郎欲语低头笑，
碧玉搔头[3]落水中。

Song of Picking Lotus Seeds

By Bai Juyi (the Tang Dynasty)

Water chestnuts and lotus sway in the breeze on the waves;

Small boats are found sailing deep into the lotus groves.

Bending her head, smiling, she's ready to speak to her lover

When the jade hairpin of hers happens to fall into the water.

注释:

①萦波:随波颤动。

②飐风:在风中摆舞。

③碧玉搔头:碧玉簪。

解读与译记:

这首《采莲曲》采用流行在江南一带的民歌的形式,极富江南水乡的风味和生活情趣。整首诗用“抓拍”的手法,记录了一位怀春的少女在跟情郎不期而遇时所表露的那种不知所措的样子。

也许是在一个风和日丽的上午,艳阳高照,清风徐徐,微风中菱叶颤动,荷叶田田摆舞;采摘莲子的青年男女都划动着小船,朝荷塘深处前进——“菱叶萦波荷飐风,荷花深处小船通”,一派生气勃勃、令人心旷神怡的景象。正在此时,她的情哥哥也出现在她有限的视野之中(因为荷叶繁茂,挡住了对面来的小船),或许是巧遇,或许是男方故意为之。这种欢喜使得姑娘手足无措:跟他搭讪呢,还是做一点更为亲昵的举动?太过于突然，少女的羞涩感很自然地使她低下头去。她不敢正视对方——那位她梦魂萦绕的意中人。谁知今天出门时可能因为匆忙，连头上的碧玉簪都不曾插紧，冷不丁地掉落在碧水之中了。

这首诗表现了一位采莲姑娘腼腆的神态和羞涩的心理。全篇语言简洁、明快，富有江南民歌的活泼、风趣的特点，犹如一幅江南水乡的风情画，也是一首朴素、生动的爱情诗。

“菱叶萦波荷飐风”这一行最不易译妥。七个字由两组主谓结构组成：菱叶萦波和荷（叶）飐风。菱叶不像荷叶能在风中摆动，只能是随波颤动，两种水生植物在微风中的“表现”是不一样的。如果一定要紧扣原文，将“颤动”和“摆动”分别来译，势必使译文拖沓，因此译成 Water chestnuts and lotus sway in the breeze on the waves。“逢郎欲语低头笑，碧玉搔头落水中”，要表达“欲语”（正当要说话……忽然间），就用了 she's ready to speak...when...happens to 的结构，来体现事情发生的或然性。

遣悲怀三首(其二)

〔唐〕元　稹

昔日戏言身后意[1]，
今朝都到眼前来。
衣裳已施行看尽，
针线犹存未忍开。
尚[2]想旧情怜婢仆，
也曾因梦送钱财。
诚知此恨人人有，
贫贱夫妻百事哀。

Expression of Sorrowful Feelings (Ⅱ)

By Yuan Zhen (the Tang Dynasty)

In the past we often talked for a joke about things after our death,

But today everything we then foresaw has become the sad truth.

Your clothes have almost been donated to others as you wished;

Your needles and threads you left behind still remain untouched.

I am kind to our old servants because of your affections for them,

And I have tried to send money to you for your request in dream.

I've truly realized that everyone has the same regret as we had

That for poor couples nothing good is worth to be mentioned.

注释：

①意：意料（会发生的事情）。

②尚：且；尚且。

解读与译记：

元稹的《遣悲怀三首》是悼念亡妻韦丛的，被称为悼亡诗的绝响。清代蘅塘退士曾赞誉："古今悼亡诗充栋，终无能出此三首范围者，勿以浅近忽之。"（《唐诗三百首》）这里选的是第二首。

从一、二两句来看，虽然他们俩属贫贱夫妻，但是感情笃厚。妻子在日，夫妻俩常常开玩笑似的设想着，如果他们当中谁先死了，情况会是怎样。不料竟一语成谶，妻子走在了元稹的前面。这首诗虽然用语平实、质朴，却是字字血、声声泪。也许，妻子生前是个贤淑而又心地善良的妇人。她曾说起，如果她先离去，就将她穿过的衣裳统统送给有需要的穷苦邻舍。妻子亡故之后，因为怕触景伤情，诗人连妻子日常曾用过的针线盒，也不敢打开来看。而且，因为两人对待家仆就像家人一样，和他们关系融洽，诗人也常常因想起妻子而怜惜仆人。妻子活着时，日子过得非常简朴甚至艰难，现在诗人竟然在梦里给妻子送去了零花钱。最后两句，道出了贫贱夫妻共同的悲惨命运：活着的时候，履穿踵决，日子过得紧巴巴的；一方死了之后，剩下的人也只能在梦中去实现曾经憧憬过的生活。贫穷的夫妻，总难逃诗中这般悲凉的结局。

笔者在译最后两句时，跟原文有少许出入：I've truly realized that everyone has the same regret as we had / That for poor couples nothing good is worth to be mentioned.（如今我真正体会到，大家都有这样共同的感叹：贫困潦倒的夫妻，家庭生活也真是乏善可陈啊！）

夜雨寄北

〔唐〕李商隐

君问归期未有期，
巴山①夜雨涨秋池。
何当②共剪西窗烛，
却话巴山夜雨时。

A Letter Home on a Rainy Night

By Li Shangyin (the Tang Dynasty)

If you ask me when I'll come home, I could only say, "Not sure."

But the autumn night downpour at Bashan is just filling pools here.

We'll soon reunite, cutting the candlewick beside the west window,

While sitting abreast, talking about what is happening at Bashan now.

注释：

①巴山：在四川省境内，南江县北。

②何当：什么时候。

解读与译记：

李商隐以诗的形式写了一封家书。诗人那时在四川巴山一带，刚好遇上连绵秋雨；从他乡夜雨联想到在家的妻儿，于是写了这首平实而又富于深情的诗。

“君问归期未有期”，这第一句中有问有答。意为妻子常常记挂着他，也许老是问他（是自问也未可知）什么时候可以回家，可是他哪里回答得了，连自己也不知道呢。何况此刻苍茫的巴山正下着滂沱的秋雨，几乎所有的池塘都满水了。接下来的两句“何当共剪西窗烛，却话巴山夜雨时”，写得婉转曲折，既有自问自答，又有满满的期待：什么时候我们能团聚呢？那样的话，我们可以肩并肩地靠在一起，慢慢地给你讲述今晚巴山下雨的情状。简单四句问答，巧妙地运用了时空的转换，用有限的篇幅揭示了无限的深情。难怪有前人评说：“眼前景反作

后日怀想，此意更深！”（清代桂馥《札朴》卷六）

这首诗用平白如话的文字，抒发诗人对爱妻的眷恋和深情；把现前实景、将来和想象中会发生的事，一桩桩一件件有条不紊地抒写出来。

“何当”二字，本表示疑问，即“什么时候”之义，这里将它译作肯定的We’ll soon reunite，也许更能给千里之外的妻子吃一颗定心丸。

标题“寄北”，说的是“寄往北面的家”，这里就直接译作A Letter Home。

无　题[1]

〔唐〕李商隐

相见时难别亦难，
东风无力百花残。
春蚕到死丝方尽，
蜡炬成灰泪始干。
晓镜但愁云鬓改，
夜吟应觉月光寒。
蓬莱[2]此去无多路，
青鸟[3]殷勤为探看。

An Untitled Song

by Li Shangyin (the Tang Dynasty)

It is hard to meet and so is to part from each other;
The east wind is weak while flowers going to wither.
Silkworms stop silk-making only when they are dying;
Until turning to ashes the candle keeps tear-shedding.
In the morn, your dark hair might turn grey in the mirror, you worry;
At night I should feel cold when I sit composing poetry.
Luckily the fairy hills are not far away from here;
I wish the blue bird would often for information go there.

注释：

①无题：无题诗，可能是因为想不出一个恰当的题目，或是有意不写明题目。李商隐多写无题诗，可能是因为他的诗写得比较朦胧、晃荡迷离，题目也让读者自己解读之后去定吧。

②蓬莱："蓬莱、方丈、瀛洲，此三神山者，其传在渤海中。"（《汉书·郊祀志》）。

③青鸟：传说是一种有三只脚的鸟，可传递书信（《史记·司马相如传》中有相关记载）。

解读与译记：

李商隐善作无题诗，常常以无题寄意。像这首无题诗，显然是一首爱情诗，以一系列意象，一层层地展现诗人对他深爱之人的思念、关爱和不离不弃的情感。

首句是直接抒情（王国维所说的"有我之境"），第二句是写景——"东风无力百花残"。可能已到暮春时节，曾经明艳一时的百花纷纷凋零。虽在写景，也暗示诗人黯然神伤的心境。三、四两句"春蚕到死丝方尽，蜡炬成灰泪始干"，表示他们之间不离不弃地相爱到永远的决心：如同春蚕一直吐丝至生命的最后一刻，要像蜡烛那样燃烧到烛泪流干方肯罢休。这是何等坚贞、执着的爱情啊！“晓镜但愁云鬓改，夜吟应觉月光寒”两句，体现了爱情的真挚，从欣赏体貌之悦过渡到对对方身体的关爱：“但愁”“应觉”等词语反映出诗人的爱有多体贴入微。诗人在关心对方的同时，也暗暗勉励自己，为了这份爱情，也要善自珍重。因此，将“晓镜”一句译成 In the morn, your dark hair might turn grey in the mirror, you worry，说的是她；而将“夜吟”这句译作 At night I should feel cold when I sit composing poetry，说的是自己。最后两句，用“蓬莱”“青鸟”等自知虚妄的东西，来排遣心中相思之苦闷；明知不可能而偏偏把希望寄托于它们，足见诗人之痴心和心境之悲凉。“蓬莱”指的是恋人所在地，实则是百分之百的“乌有乡”；“青鸟”曾为王母当过信使，它真也能为诗人来做这差事？理想和想象极其“丰满”，而现实又是多么渺茫和虚无！所谓“殷勤为探看”，也不过是自欺欺人，为了得到暂时的精神解脱罢了。这样的爱情，是何等炽烈，又是何等苦涩和悲伤！

寄　人

〔唐〕张　泌

别梦依依到谢家①，
小廊回合②曲阑斜。
多情只有春庭月，
犹为离人照落花。

A Message

By Zhang Bi (the Tang Dynasty)

Since our separation I have often dreamed as if I were in your residence,

Where the veranda was winding and the balustrade slanting as ever.

In the yard the spring moon seemed to be the only thing affectionate and tender,
Which was shedding light on the fallen petals for my love's absence.

注释：

①谢家：代指女子的家，盖以东晋才女谢道韫借称其人。

②回合：缭绕；环绕。

解读与译记：

这是一首伤别离的诗，说白一点，是一首记录诗人或某个男子失恋的诗。“别梦依依到谢家，小廊回合曲阑斜”，意思是自从跟心爱的女友分别（也许是分手）之后，几乎夜不能成寐，睡着了又每每梦见原先热恋的日子。这里的“依依”除了展示梦里依稀、隐约的情状之外，也表达难舍难分的依恋之情。每次都梦见在女方的家里，两人手牵着手，在曲折的回廊里走走停停，一会儿凭栏观看池子里养着的游鱼，一会儿又相依而坐，窃窃私语。那是何等浪漫和销魂的日子！可如今你径自离开了我，杳无音信，我简直失魂落魄，茶饭不思。

前两句诗写的是对别后梦境的回忆，而这后两句写的是眼前所见的实况——“多情只有春庭月，犹为离人照落花”——语中充满嗔怪和怨艾，意思是：你呀，真的太狠心了，把我生生地丢下，独自离去。你还不及眼前春天庭院里的月色，它依然跟往昔一样，慷慨地临照着满园的落英，仿佛还记得我们以往在一起时的春天。只是如今物是人非，你竟一去杳如黄鹤，怎能不让我心碎呢?

译文在第一句里用了 as if，在第二句里用了 as ever，来表达主人公恍恍惚惚好像回到了女子的家；而在他眼前，庭院依旧、回廊犹在，却怎么也见不到女子本人，怅然之意，溢于言表。“谢家”，代指女子的家，盖以东晋才女谢道韫借称其人。从“多情只有春庭月，犹为离人照落花”两句可知，诗人微微埋怨甚至嗔怪“她”了。这里把“多情”译作 affectionate and tender，把“离人”译作 my love’s absence（心爱之人的缺席），来传达诗人幽怨婉转的情感。

采莲子二首（其二）

〔唐〕皇甫松

船动湖光滟滟[1]秋，
贪看年少[2]信[3]船流。
无端[4]隔水抛莲子，
遥被人知半日羞。

Song of Picking Lotus Seeds (Ⅱ)

By Huangfu Song (the Tang Dynasty)

On an autumn day the boat moves on the lake with water shimmering,

Covetously looking at the boy, she lets her boat go with current floating.

She throws lotus seeds to him in the neighboring boat without hesitation,

And afraid of being noticed, she's ashamed of herself for long then.

注释：

①滟滟：水波粼粼。

②年少：少年。

③信：随意，由之。

④无端：无缘无故。

解读与译记：

本诗生动记录了一位质朴率真的少女主动追求爱慕的少年的场面。

天高云淡的秋日，湖面波光粼粼，采集莲子的小船在荷叶丛中来回穿梭。此时一艘船上的一位采莲少女，忽然瞧见不远处的船上有一翩翩少年；她痴痴地盯着他，竟然忘记驾驭自己的小船，由它随波漂流。见那美少年并不曾注意自己，她情急之下，抓起一把莲子，朝着他扔了过去。她猛然醒悟，自己的举动失之轻浮，甚至太过鲁莽，下意识地低下头去。少女的羞涩使她脸红耳赤，让她半天也抬不起头来。要是这一举动被人瞧见如何是好？羞怯和懊悔交织在一起，让她久久难以释怀。

第二句中的“贪”字极为传神，把少女那种追求爱情的迫切心情，鲜活地显现于纸上。译作 covetously，是否能传达原作的意思，有待读者检验。另一“遥”字，很难译妥，所以在上下文中增加 afraid of being noticed 和 for long then 来使译文更清晰准确。

忆扬州

〔唐〕徐　凝

萧娘①脸薄难胜泪，

桃叶②眉长易觉愁。

天下三分明月夜，

二分无赖③是扬州。

Recalling Yangzhou

By Xu Ning (the Tang Dynasty)

Her face is too tender to bear stains of sad tears;

Her long brows remind me of the sorrow she suffers.

Of the beautiful moonlit night today, for no reason,

More than half belongs to Yangzhou which she is in.

注释：

①萧娘：诗词中通常指男子所恋的女子。女子所恋的男子则被称为“萧郎”。

②桃叶：原指王献之爱妾，后常用作咏歌妓的典故。这里还是指第一句里的“萧娘”。

③无赖：因情绪无所依托而发出的一种痴情抱怨。

解读与译记：

寓情于景的诗词作品，在我国文学宝库中不胜枚举。这首《忆扬州》就是其中脍炙人口的作品之一。在唐代，扬州是商贾云集、美女遍地之所，诗人赞美它可以有无数理由，但他却用了一半的篇幅来写扬州的月：“天下三分明月夜，二分无赖是扬州。”

月亮这一意象，在我国古典诗歌里，是一位出镜频率非常高的“大腕”：它可以表达乡愁，可以象征团圆，可以暗示永恒……诗人在这里，明显是用它来寄托相思。也许，是在一个明月朗照之夜，诗人见月思人，才写下这流传千古的美丽而忧伤的诗行。

我们可以这样设想：难忘啊，难忘的是我们分别时的情景。我那心爱的人，当时哭成了一个泪人，搭着我的肩膀，怎么也不让我离去。我走之后，我猜得到你整天是紧锁双眉，愁云不散。你一定想象得出，因为我们目前天各一方，我会有多想你！像这样皓月临照的美丽夜晚，咱俩本该偎依在一起，共同享受这美景良辰。这柔情万种的月色，我多么愿意统统都给了你。而我也只是凡夫俗子，根本做不到呀。但是，在此时此刻我的心里，这月色至少一大半应该献给你！可是这能做到吗？不过这念头总在我心头挥之不去啊！

“萧娘”“桃叶”在此处采用意译；不仅因为直译有难度，而且在这首诗里，它们对展示诗歌的意境作用不大，因为诗人在写诗的时候也只是为了“掉书袋”而已，所以，译作her更干净利落。“脸薄”和“眉长”本是用来勾画他爱人的容貌，这里面自然夹带着个人的感情。因此译作Her face is too tender to bear stains of sad tears和Her long brows remind me of the sorrow she suffers。把这些感情，分别让sad tears, the sorrow she suffers来承担。

“天下三分明月夜，二分无赖是扬州”是千古名句，男女老少耳熟能详。如果将“二分”机械地译作two thirds，貌似忠实，实则方枘圆凿、焚琴煮鹤矣。译成现在这样，传达了其中意思：Of the beautiful moonlit night today, for no reason, / More than half belongs to Yangzhou which she is in 。有了which she is in，才能真正体现“怀地”完全是为了“怀人”。“无赖”译成for no reason（无端），有一种热恋者自怨自艾、怨天尤人的意味。

蝶恋花（庭院深深深几许）

〔北宋〕欧阳修

庭院深深深几许？
杨柳堆烟①，帘幕无重数。
玉勒雕鞍②游冶处，
楼高不见章台③路。

雨横④风狂三月暮，
门掩黄昏，无计留春住。
泪眼问花花不语，
乱红飞过秋千去。

Love of Butterfly

By Ouyang Xiu (the Northern Song Dynasty)

The courtyard is so deep, but how deep whoever knows ?
It is in the mist-clouded willows, and hidden by screen after screen.
On his jade-inlaid saddle he's gone to his haunt, merry making;
Although she's on the high tower, she can't see him now pleasure pursuing.

It is late March with a stiff wind and a torrential rain;
Dusk is shut by the gate within, but that can by no means detain spring.
All tears she asks the flowers why, yet silent they remain;
In a riot of petals, they fly over the swing.

注释:

①杨柳堆烟:杨柳被浓浓的烟雾笼罩着。

②玉勒雕鞍:镶玉的马笼头和雕花的马鞍。这里代指马车。

③章台:汉代长安的章台街,是妓院聚集之地。

④横:凶暴。

解读与译记:

“庭院深深深几许?”这个问句表明闺中人所在庭院之幽深和僻静,谁也不知它究竟有多幽深(或是:这庭院实在太过幽静了)。接连用了三个“深”字,从形式上就夺人眼球,让人产生一种非得往下读的好奇和冲动。果不其然,下面的“杨柳堆烟,帘幕无重数”,更进一步写明闺中人被“深锁”豪门庭院的寂寞处境。宅院四周遍布柳树,而柳树上的晨雾又如烟雾般笼罩,还有那一重更比一重深的帘幕,遮挡得让人透不过气来。闺中少妇正当花样年华,可是她丈夫却是个不着家的花花公子,他此刻身在何处?“玉勒雕鞍游冶处,楼高不见章台路”,丈夫整天花天酒地,热衷寻花问柳。他骑着玉勒雕鞍的马,正往他常去的烟花柳巷作乐寻欢呢。丈夫的心,早已不属于她了,只得由他去吧!

“雨横风狂三月暮,门掩黄昏,无计留春住”:此时正值三月末,曾惊艳一时的繁花先后凋零,何况又遇上这无情的狂风暴雨,更是落红无数。主人公在大自然面前又能怎样呢?只得把门关得紧紧的，也许是不让狂风施虐，又有留住春天之意，用语双关。但尽管她努力过了，可又怎能留得住春天，留得住自己如花的年华？

在百无聊赖中，她步出房门，来到庭院。她见到被狂风暴雨施虐过的花树，落红遍地，伤春之情油然而生。触景伤情，悲从中来；挂着热泪，以满满的同情心低头问候遍地落英。可谁知“落花有意，流水无情”，像是有意在气她，花瓣们随着一阵大风飞舞到秋千那边去了！

这“泪眼问花花不语，乱红飞过秋千去”两句，被王国维先生当作“有我之境”之著例，其他诗词评论家也常常加以引用。这位被冷落于深闺的佳人，含着泪水在问花：为何自己会留不住爱人、留不住青春呢？可是，落花毕竟无情，甚至连理会一声都不愿意，径自随风飘舞到秋千那边去了（All tears she asks the flowers why, yet silent they remain; / In a riot of petals, they fly over the swing）。这算是一种反衬，以乐写哀吧？

“庭院深深深几许？”这里连续用了三个“深”字，其语法功能不同，仔细一想，的确出手不凡。笔者用 The courtyard is so deep, but how deep whoever knows 来传达，不知能否差强人意？“游冶”指“流连妓院，追逐声色”，译作 he's gone to his haunt, merry-making，委婉程度与原文相近。同样“章台路”也做这样处理，译为 pleasure-pursuing。用 a riot of petals 来表达落花的无情，径自在一阵欢闹中飞跃过秋千。

江城子·乙卯正月二十日夜记梦

〔北宋〕苏轼

十年生死两茫茫[1]，

不思量，

自难忘。

千里孤坟，

无处话凄凉。

纵使相逢应不识，

尘满面，

鬓如霜。

夜来幽梦忽还乡，

River Town:

A Dream of My Deceased Wife on the 20th of the First Lunar Month in 1075

By Su Shi (the Northern Song Dynasty)

I've been empty and you, inaccessible since your death ten years ago:

Trying hard not to think of you,

But how could I forget you?

Your lonely tomb is thousands of miles away,

So I've got nobody to pour out my sorrow.

Even if we met now, for sure, we wouldn't recognize each other:

For my face is dust-worn

And my temples going grey.

Last night I dreamed that I seemed our home to go;

小轩窗，

正梳妆。

相顾无言，

惟有泪千行。

料得年年肠断处，

明月夜，

短松冈[2]。

I saw you stand as usual by the little window

Doing up your hair.

We looked at each other speechless,

Only torrential tears rolling down our cheeks.

I presume how broken-hearted you would be this time every year

In your grave bathed in the moonlight,

On a knoll overgrown with short pines on a quiet night.

注释：

①茫茫：空虚渺茫的样子。

②短松冈：指妻子的墓地所在，长满松树的小山冈。

解读与译记：

苏轼的诗词，给人的印象向来是雄文大手挥写豪迈之情，其实他也可以用平实、朴素的笔墨来抒发幽深细腻的情感。这首《江城子·乙卯正月二十日夜记梦》就属于后者。

这是他悼念亡妻王弗之作，写于她谢世后十年，表达对爱妻深深的思念之情。“十年生死两茫茫，不思量，自难忘。”十年了，夫妻俩阴阳两隔；虽然尽量不去想她，但是妻子在时，夫妻俩琴瑟相和的生活怎么能说忘就忘得了呢？朴实的语言里，透露出对亡妻深深的哀思和无言的伤痛。“不思量”，并不是真正意义上“不想她”，一是因为老夫子自身政务繁忙，且仕途不畅，使得他无暇顾及“思量”，更为重要的是因为他采用了思想上的逃避法。这是丧亲之人常用的缓解痛苦的方法之一。

“千里孤坟，无处话凄凉。”妻子王氏安葬在四川老家，孑然孤坟，又离他任上所在的山东路途遥远，因此他即便有万语千言要向她倾诉，也无法实现。十年了，岁月消磨，政事烦心，对她的思念却与日俱增。这一切使得他忽然感到自己老了不少："纵使相逢应不识，尘满面，鬓如霜。"

下阕写的是跟妻子在梦里相见的情景。"夜来幽梦忽还乡，小轩窗，正梳妆"，正所谓日有所思夜有所梦，词人在梦里依稀回到了妻子活着的时日。此刻看到妻子跟以往一样，正在窗前悉心打扮自己；那身影是多么熟悉和亲切呀！不料她蓦然回首，两人目光对视的刹那，竟然无言可说，双方只有相视伫立、泪雨滂沱。

理智又使他回到了现实。他觉得，跟妻子已经阴阳永隔，真正团聚只有在梦中。现在他只能每年在明月朗照的夜晚，在长满松树的小山冈上，对着妻子的墓独自断肠。

"十年生死两茫茫"是千古名句，可是要译成另一种文字，却难倒译者了。"两茫茫"里"茫茫"二字可以理解为：双方阴阳两隔，所距岂止千山万水；也可理解成苏轼因妻子故去而觉得惆怅、空茫，显得无所寄托、无从依凭。其实，这"两"字仅仅是存在于词人头脑中的幻想；人一旦死去，一切归于空茫，故也谈不上"一"或"两"。说是"两茫茫"，实际上只是他独自的感受罢了。因此，这里译作 I've been empty and you, inaccessible since your death ten years ago（十年了，你的逝去使我心境空虚，你又杳无音信）。译文仅说生者和亡魂之间无法交流，其中还应包含生者的感受——怅然若失、无所依凭。因此，这显然不是最佳的处理办法，此乃不得已而为之。

悼亡三首(其二)

〔北宋〕梅尧臣

每出身如梦，

逢人强意[1]多。

归来仍寂寞，

欲语向谁何？

窗冷孤萤入，

宵长一雁过。

世间无最苦，

精爽[2]此销磨。

Song of Condolence (Ⅱ)

By Mei Yaochen (the Northern Song Dynasty)

Every time I leave home I feel as if in dream;

A forced "hello" to acquaintances is what I can do.

I feel even more lonely when I'm back home;

Can I tell whatever sad in my heart to you?

At night fireflies happen to dash into my window cold;

And a lonely wild goose chances to fly by, crying.

If you ask me whatever is the bitterest in this world,

Nothing but my fate is most spiritual consuming.

注释：

①强意：勉强应付。

②精爽：精神状态。

解读与译记：

梅尧臣中年时，妻子谢氏在一次旅途中暴亡，因家境贫寒，连归葬她也无能为力。在感慨伤怀中，他写下《悼亡三首》以怀念妻子。这里选的是第二首。

大凡经历过中年丧妻的人，都会有这首诗中的感受。夫妻俩生活了半辈子，突然另一半溘然长逝，这种在精神上的打击不啻晴天霹雳。诗人整天精神恍惚，如在梦中。外出时，碰到了熟人，也只是点个头或是说声“你好”，不过是强作应付罢了。回到家中，看到家里一切依旧，只是昔日朝夕与共、相濡以沫的妻子已经不在了；阴阳暌隔，情何以堪！最为难捱的时候是晚上，夜深人静，辗转反侧、孤枕难眠。夜半三更，飞经屋顶的孤雁一声鸣叫，或是无意中闯入的一只飞萤，都增加了他形影相吊的思绪。人世间伤心的经历多多，但是在诗人看来，莫过于丧妻带来的这种痛苦和折磨：夜以继日、镂心刻骨的追思，触景伤情、萧索落寞的独守，即便有再好的身体，也经受不了这无穷尽的精神折磨啊！

“逢人强意多”此处译作A forced “hello” to acquaintances is what I can do。外出时碰到的熟人，也只有强打精神，说声“你好”。“欲语向谁何？”分明是：我心里有千万的苦衷，除了你之外，又能跟谁去诉说呢(Can I tell whatever sad in my heart to you)?“世间无最苦”，也就是“世间最为痛心的事，也就莫过于此”(If you ask me whatever is the bitterest in this world)。“精爽此销磨”当中的“此”字译成my fate，也许更能体现诗人的不幸遭遇。

钗头凤(红酥手)

〔南宋〕陆　游

红酥手,黄縢[1] 酒。
满城春色宫墙[2]柳。
东风[3]恶,欢情薄。
一怀愁绪,几年离索[4]。
错,错,错。

春如旧,人空瘦。
泪痕红浥[5]鲛绡[6]透。
桃花落,闲池阁[7]。
山盟[8]虽在,锦书[9]难托。
莫,莫,莫[10]!

Phoenix Hairpin

By Lu You (the Southern Song Dynasty)

Never can I forget how you toasted me top-grade wine with your rosy and tender hands,
While in the garden, filled with the charm of spring, the palace willows tall and green.
The east wind was so hateful that it broke up our sweet marriage life,
And broken-hearted, we've lived a desolate and lonely life these years.
How regretful I am, and absolutely regretful!

Spring comes again, beautiful as ever, yet you, my dear, are pining for me to no avail.
Your tears've been washing away your rouge on cheeks, with your silk handkerchief wet through.
Peach flower petals are scattered everywhere, pools dry, pavilions and towers deserted.
Our vows for eternal love are still in our hearts, but in what way can I deliver to you my kerchief letter?
Ah, let all this go, and go for ever!

注释:

①黄縢:指美酒。宋代官酒以黄纸为封,黄封酒代指美酒。

②宫墙:南宋以绍兴为陪都,绍兴城内的某些园林的高墙,亦可称为宫墙。

③东风:暗指陆游的母亲。

④离索:离群索居。

⑤浥:弄湿。

⑥鲛绡:这里指手帕。绡,生丝,生丝织物。

⑦池阁:池上的楼阁。

⑧山盟:旧时常用山盟海誓,对山立盟,指海起誓。

⑨锦书:写在锦上的书信。

⑩莫、莫、莫:罢了。

解读与译记:

这首《钗头凤》,使陆游与唐琬的爱情悲剧,成为家喻户晓的凄美故事。

上阕是陆游回忆与唐琬婚后的那一段美好的夫妻生活。

陆游选取了一桩非常有代表性的往事来抒写他们曾经琴瑟和谐、相敬如宾的美好时光。两人在南宋陪都绍兴的沈园相偕春游,在游乐的间隙,坐下来把酒言欢。当时的唐琬是何等风姿绰约、婉婳动人。请看她举杯给丈夫敬酒时伸出的手,是那么红润细腻;而所饮的酒也是最为上乘的黄封佳酿。在春色满园、柳树垂青的环境下,这对饮着酒的恩爱夫妻万万没想到,他们的幸福生活正迈向尽头。陆游的母亲,竟要求陆游休掉妻子唐琬。出于对母亲的"孝顺"或屈服于她的淫威,陆游休掉了妻子。这不啻一个晴天霹雳,好端端的一对夫妻就这样被拆散了。在嗣后的数年间,彼此间杳无音信,各自在无尽的思念中遭受痛苦折磨。"东风恶"一语双关,字面上是说,猛烈的东风将满眼的繁花吹得七零八落,实际上则是影射陆母太过狠心,将这对天作之合给生生地拆散了。陆游想到过劝说母亲,可他的懦弱性格使他踌躇不前。母命难违啊!但后悔呀,真是连肠子都悔青了!

多年后,陆游跟唐琬在沈园不期而遇;此时的唐琬已经嫁与他人。春色依然,沈园如旧,可是眼前的唐琬,跟当年已经判若两人:精神折磨摧垮了她的形貌——憔悴不堪、形容枯槁。回忆起往昔在一起和美的婚姻生活,唐琬怆然涕下,哭得像泪人一般,致使胭红掉落,丝帕湿透。春色将逝,落红遍地;池水枯竭,亭台寂寞。此时的陆游,对唐琬还是一往情深,而后者又何尝不是心中满是愿比翼双飞的鸟儿、直至地久天长的誓言呢？但是，虽有千言万语要向对方表白，可这一帕情书，又有谁来替他们传递呢？算了吧，算了吧！所有这一切竟然已成明日黄花，悔之晚矣！

“红酥手，黄縢酒”，国内读者在解读上，应该不会太困难。因为，在中国古典诗词的熏陶下，国人很适应这种遣词造句的习惯：跳跃、生动，追求形式和音韵上的美感。此处的“红”与“黄”，讲究色彩的对照。红润纤细的手，与黄封的佳酿，也相辅相成地营造出一种和谐的意境。可是对于英文读者，如果依葫芦画瓢地译成red tender hands和yellow-sealed wine，也许会使他们云里雾里，摸不着头脑。笔者将其译成Never can I forget how you toasted me top-grade wine with your rosy and tender hands，也许会容易让他们接受。再如，“错，错，错”，笔者没有译成Wrong, wrong, wrong，而是译作How regretful I am, and absolutely regretful，表示诗人的深深悔意。“莫，莫，莫”，也用同样方法处理：Ah, let all this go, and go for ever! 罢了，罢了！因为为时已晚！

在中国古典诗词翻译中，如何再现典故或展显诗词的背景这一棘手问题，经常会碰到。像这首词中的“东风恶”暗指陆母对陆游夫妇婚姻生活的干涉，使得他们分手。即便是国内读者，如果没有老师或书本的帮助，也不能一眼就能看出“东风”是指陆母。笔者在这里用了依样画葫芦的办法，直接译作The east wind was so hateful that it broke up our sweet marriage life。读者一定会提出这样的疑问:东风究竟有什么样的能力,竟然能拆散好端端的一对夫妻?英文读者一脸狐疑:How?而国内的读者除了有书本和老师的帮助之外,还可以从自己的文化基因里找到解开问题的钥匙,因为接下来的“桃花落,闲池阁”等意象会帮其慢慢悟出东风所指。可惜,英文读者看了译文,根本无从知道这“东风恶”跟陆游夫妻离散有什么瓜葛。这确实是笔者学力不逮所致。这里只能将其作为问题顺便提一下,并期待着后来的译者能处理得更好。

青玉案·元夕[1]

〔南宋〕辛弃疾

东风夜放花千树[2]。

更吹落，星如雨[3]。

宝马雕车[4]香满路。

凤箫[5]声动，玉壶[6]光转，一夜鱼龙[7]舞。

蛾儿雪柳黄金缕，[8]

笑语盈盈[9]暗香去。

众里寻他[10]千百度[11]，

蓦然[12]回首，那人却在，灯火阑珊[13]处。

Green Jade Cup:

Lantern Festival Night

By Xin Qiji (the Southern Song Dynasty)

At night myriad lanterns in a riot of color seem as if blossoms stirred by the east wind
And fireworks are let off and fall like a rain of stars.

Proud horses with decorated carriages behind are seen leaving all the way a trace of scent;
Phoenix flutes blowing, the moon moving, dragon-and-fish lantern dancers perform all night.

With ornaments of moth-like and leave-shaped hairpins,

Graceful women in groups go past with giggles and a faint fragrance.
In the surging crowd, I look for her time and time again but almost in vain,
Yet, as I suddenly look around, I see her, who is in the spot which is least lighted.

注释：

①元夕：旧历正月十五元宵节，是夜称元夕或元夜。

②花千树：花灯多得像千树开花。

③星如雨：指焰火纷纷，像雨点似的落下。

④宝马雕车：装饰华丽的马车。

⑤凤箫：排箫，箫管排列参差如凤翼，故名。

⑥玉壶：比喻月亮。

⑦鱼龙：指鱼灯与龙灯。

⑧蛾儿雪柳黄金缕：蛾儿、雪柳、黄金缕皆为古代妇女的首饰，有各种形状和质地。这里指盛装的妇女们。

⑨盈盈：形容女子仪态美好。

⑩他：泛指第三人称，古时，“他”与“她”不分。

⑪千百度：反反复复，千百遍。

⑫蓦然：忽然。

⑬灯火阑珊：指灯火幽微、稀少。

解读与译记：

这首《青玉案·元夕》，上阕写元宵节灯会的盛况。

上元节晚上，在灯会现场上，那些形形色色、多姿多彩的花灯，在烟火的衬托下，仿佛被一夜东风吹开了的千万簇花朵。烟火时不时地出现在空中，像漫天繁星被吹落了。豪华马车来往穿梭在街道上；熙熙攘攘的人群里，弥漫着阵阵幽微香气。不绝于耳的排箫声，在夜晚的空气中悠悠回荡。圆月当空，时光在欢声笑语中流逝；舞动龙灯和鱼灯的人们，通宵达旦，尽情地挥舞着、欢笑着，意犹未尽。姑娘们正值花样年华，难得在一年一度的灯会上展示一下自己，于是都悉心打扮：衣裳花色繁多、剪裁合体，头上的饰品也形态各异，晶莹剔透，在流光的映照下轻轻晃动，格外引人注目。姑娘们边走边观赏灯会，不时发出一阵阵清脆的笑声。婀娜多姿的背影，留下了缕缕幽幽的馨香，久久不能散去。

下阕笔锋一转，离开了万众同乐的闹元宵盛况，词人写自己在专心致志地寻找一个人；尽管千百遍地在万头攒动、摩肩接踵的人群中寻找，却总是无果而终。正当他怅然若失之际，猛然回头，却发现自己要找的那个“她”，正一个人静静地待在灯火幽微的地方！

从该词作的构思上看，上下阕分量有些失衡。很显然，诗人用大量篇幅来描述上元节灯会的盛况，其真实目的是突出下阕他找人的专注和辛苦。词人其实对灯会的炫目和人群的欢闹都心不在焉,他的心中只有那个“她”。这也许是词人来到现场的唯一目的。或许他们事先约好要在灯会上幽会,但女方又没有跟他商定在何处见面;或许是那女孩在考验词人的诚意;又或许这本身就是一场男子忘情地追求女子的喜剧。这样看来,词人在上阕的所有笔墨,都是在为约会做铺垫,更展现了真正的爱情来之不易的道理。

“众里寻他千百度”,如果要强调看灯会的人群之众,那在crowd前面加上surging,更能体现观灯的人越来越多,所以,即便千百次地寻找,也很难有结果。“千百度”译成time and time again,笔者还觉得不够分量,于是加上almost in vain。“阑珊”译作least lighted,不知是否更接近原文的意思。

王国维在《人间词话》中说“成就一切事,罔不历三种境界”,第三境即最终境界才至“众里寻他千百度,蓦然回首,那人却在,灯火阑珊处”。而前两种境界分别是“昨夜西风凋碧树。独上西楼,望尽天涯路”(北宋晏殊《蝶恋花(槛菊愁烟兰泣露)》)与“为伊消得人憔悴,衣带渐宽终不悔”(北宋柳永《蝶恋花(伫倚危楼风细细)》)。笔者发现,无论是《人间词话》里说的三种境界还是本首词作,前部都有“苦苦寻求”的过程,到了最后才柳暗花明,豁然开朗,有个明显的转折。如果把重点放在“蓦然回首”和“却”上,可以从一个不常见的角度来理解整首词:“东风夜放花千树”“一夜鱼龙舞”是何等繁盛浮华。年少轻狂，谁不曾被膏粱锦绣迷住双眼，一路踌躇满志，寻寻觅觅，或贪或嗔或痴，参不透、求不得，辗转反侧。要经过多少蹉跎，才能“蓦然回首”，才能转念或者顿悟，发觉那“灯火阑珊处”的平凡爱意才是珍宝。芸芸众生，惊天动地是为少，平平凡凡才是真，愿得一份质朴的欢喜之情，而不是留下“当时只道是寻常”（清代纳兰性德《浣溪沙（谁念西风独自凉）》）的遗憾。

摸鱼儿·雁丘词

〔金〕元好问

乙丑岁赴试并州，道逢捕雁者云："今旦获一雁，杀之矣。其脱网者悲鸣不能去，竟自投于地而死。"予因买得之，葬之汾水之上，垒石为识，号曰"雁丘"。同行者多为赋诗，予亦有《雁丘词》。旧所作无宫商，今改定之。

问世间、情是何物，

直教[①]生死相许[②]？

天南地北双飞客[③]，老翅几回寒暑。

Groping for Fish:

Song of the Wild Geese Grave

By Yuan Haowen (the Jin Dynasty)

Years ago, on my way to an examination at Bingzhou, I happened to hear that a wild goose catcher caught and killed a prey (presumably, a male wild goose). While the escaped one (maybe, the killed one's mate) chose to commit suicide by throwing herself to the ground. I bought them and buried them on the Fen River, and marked the grave by setting up a stone named "Grave of a Pair of Wild Geese". Many of my travel companions composed poems to mourn for them. I wrote a poem, *Song of the Wild Geese Grave*. The original manuscript is without prosody, and the present one is the final text.

Could you all please tell me: what on earth is true love

That makes two wild geese hold together in life and death?

Side by side, they two flew many a year despite of summer and winter,

欢乐趣，离别苦，

就中[4]更有痴儿女。

君应有语[5]，渺万里层云，

千山暮雪，只影向谁去？

横汾[6]路，

寂寞当年箫鼓[7]，荒烟依旧平楚[8]。

招魂楚些[9]何嗟及[10]，

山鬼[11]暗啼[12]风雨。

天也妒[13]，未信与，

莺儿燕子俱黄土。

千秋万古，为留待骚人[14]，

狂歌痛饮，来访雁丘处。

They enjoyed the happiness of union, suffered the bitterness of separation

With the same passionate love as people do.

Once widowed, the wild goose asked herself:

"Where should I fly all alone, through white depths and over mountains of snows at dusk?"

The riverside where the geese have been buried

Will no longer witness the noisy scenes as those years; bushes are still lush as ever.
Nobody is able to call back the spirits;

Even the mountain spirits are also wailing for them in wind and rain.

Don't you believe: Such a sad scene'll truly make Heaven envious of them?
Unlike common orioles and sparrows, they'll never be reduced to a handful of dirt.
For ages to come, poets'll surely come to the grave to condole over the geese's spirits
And sing over cups of wine instead of weeping to show their sympathy and grief.

注释:

①直教:竟使。

②许:相随。

③双飞客:指双宿双飞,秋去春来的大雁。

④就中:雁群中。

⑤君应有语:你一定会自问。

⑥横汾:指葬雁的汾水之滨。

⑦寂寞当年箫鼓:当年汉武帝横渡时场面热闹非凡,如今却寂寞凄凉。

⑧平楚:楚指丛木。远望树梢齐平,故称平楚。

⑨些(suò):语尾助词,相当于民歌中的“啰”。

⑩何嗟及:悲叹也无济于事。

⑪山鬼:《楚辞·九歌·山鬼》篇中指山神,此处指雁魂。

⑫暗啼:一作“自啼”。

⑬天也妒:上天也羡慕。

⑭骚人:诗人。

解读与译记：

这是一首咏物词，歌颂一只为自己的至爱而殉情的大雁。

词作一开头，作者就“先声夺人”，劈头就问：“问世间、情是何物，直教生死相许？”这一问好像是针对世人，但往下读，才知道作者要歌颂的是一只为自己爱侣殉情的大雁。词人提醒我们：不要以为只有人类夫妻才有相濡以沫、生死与共的情感，就连飞鸟（大雁）也有同样的情感。一旦结为连理，大雁就生死相依：无论是南来北往千万里路程，还是冬寒夏暑风餐露宿，夫妻俩肩并肩地飞翔迁徙。它们懂得双宿双飞的喜悦，更饱尝哪怕是暂时离别的痛苦和眷恋。人们总以为，只有人世间才有痴男怨女，殊不知这里说的大雁竟会为曾经形影不离的爱侣意外亡故而毅然决定殉情——坠地而死！做出如此让人匪夷所思的决定，绝对不是出于一时冲动。丈夫（我们姑且假设被杀的是雄雁）不在了，自己孤身一人、形单影只，怎样才能像过去那样去跨越万水千山、经历晨风暮雪？那时毕竟有爱侣的呵护和陪伴啊！与其孤孤单单地苟活，倒不如一头扎到地上随丈夫而去。

诚如作者的小序中所说：“其脱网者悲鸣不能去，竟自投于地而死。”这儿的脱网者，也就是这只雌雁，她终于随丈夫去了——坠地而亡。作者被雌雁的殉情壮举所感动，把这一对大雁的遗骸葬于汾水之滨。这一带是当年汉武帝渡汾河祀汾阴的地方。当时的场面有多壮观、热闹:喧天的箫鼓,动地的棹歌,而今却是平林漠漠,衰草寒烟,一派萧索凄凉。武帝早已成为过往,招魂也无济于事。这里作者只是以武帝的死来比拟大雁殉情而亡;逝者如斯,山神枉自悲啼,而死者却再也不能死而复生了!这一对大雁生死相许的深情连上天也羡慕啊。诗人深信,这对深情的大雁绝不会跟普通的莺儿、燕子那样,死后仅仅化为一抔黄土,而是将会赢得生前身后名,与日月同辉。后来的文人骚客,也一定会来寻访雁丘坟故地,狂歌痛饮,祭奠这为“至情”而赴死的亡灵。

这首词有较多的腾挪跌宕,加之引用典故,理解起来不是很容易。幸好有词人的小序,从中可以找到理解的脉络。比如上阕里的“君应有语”中的“君”是指谁,这是需要理解的关键词。这里释为,殉情的雌雁在看到丈夫的死之后的心理活动。这样才能从逻辑上将上下阕连在一起。因为雄雁意外被杀,雌雁痛不欲生;接二连三地问自己:今后孤身一人、形单影只,将如何苟活于世呢?

对于下阕的“横汾路,寂寞当年箫鼓,荒烟依旧平楚”的理解,也是从小序中觅到了解开的钥匙。原来这殉情的大雁是被埋葬在汾水之滨的,那么下面的“招魂楚些何嗟及,山鬼暗啼风雨”等等也都能够理解了。

翻译的前提是厘清以上所说的脉络,否则连英语的主语也无从知晓,更谈不上从何处着手。笔者把殉情的大雁确定为雌雁(she),这样整篇译文就找到了切入点。

从“天南地北”到“只影向谁去”,笔者用过去时来翻译。这是这对大雁夫妻活着时候的情状以及丈夫死后殉情者(martyr goose)的心理活动。

至于词中汉武帝的典故,笔者没有直接翻译出来。一来,如果大费周章地提及汉武帝当年在汾河祀汾阴的盛况,无疑会影响译文的连贯性;二来,词人引用此典故的目的,也仅仅是想渲染时过境迁所带来的寂寞和寥落。花篇幅还原典故,就显得喧宾夺主了。

“未信与”,笔者译作 don’t you believe,意为“信不信由你”。“山鬼”,译作 mountain spirits。

寄衣曲三首(其三)

〔南宋〕罗与之

此身傥①长在，

敢恨②归无日。

但愿郎防边，

似妾缝衣密。

Song of Sending Clothes (Ⅲ)

By Luo Yuzhi (the Southern Song Dynasty)

As long as I am ever alive safe and sound,

I can never complain you're away on guard.

How I wish the frontier you're guarding

Were as tight defended as my tight stitching.

注释：

①傥：如果，表示假设。

②敢恨：实为“不敢恨”。

解读与译记：

丈夫去了边防服役，妻子对他的牵挂总是不日不月的：天热了，只怕他晒着；天寒了，又深忧他冻着。这首小诗的女主人公也不例外，她作为“军嫂”，爱丈夫，也识大体。

丈夫离家长久了，难免为自己“空房难独守”而有所抱怨。但是，她抱怨归抱怨，对丈夫感情始终如一，天地可鉴，并且发誓：“此身傥长在，敢恨归无日。”即便等到地老天荒，也要盼着丈夫回来团聚。而且，常常把她对丈夫的爱，付诸实际行动，同时还在精神上支持丈夫安心服役，叮嘱丈夫要恪尽职守，把边防铸成铜墙铁壁：“但愿郎防边，似妾缝衣密。”也许，当时她正为丈夫缝寒衣呢。

要丈夫把边关守得密不透风，连一只鸟儿也飞不进来。有这样的思想高度，这位军嫂算得上是女中豪杰，令人钦佩。翻译最后这两句，边防守得牢，跟针脚缝得密，分别用 tight defended 和 tight stitching，意思表达确切，韵律也相当和谐。

相　思

〔元〕杨维桢

深情长是暗相随，
月白风清苦苦思。
不似东姑[1]痴醉酒，
幕天席地[2]了[3]无知。

Love-Sickness

By Yang Weizhen (the Yuan Dynasty)

Deep love is as close with me as a tailing shadow;

A breezy moonlit night worsens this deep sorrow.

How I envy my simple-minded neighboring maiden,

To whom everything sad will be soon cleanly forgotten.

注释:

①东姑:邻村的姑娘。

②幕天席地:以天为幕,以地当席,形容一个人无忧无虑,心胸宽大。

③了:完全。

解读与译记:

又是一支描写坠入情网的姑娘自怨自艾的相思曲。

在封建社会,女子单相思是一桩非常折磨人的事,那种情丝,可谓“剪不断理还乱”,还有那无休无止的思念与没有时日的等待。女子单恋就像是端着一杯苦涩的酒,只能独自暗暗品味。特别是在月白风清的夜晚,撩人的月色更容易使人联想到,假如能跟自己心爱的人漫步在花前月下,定会有说不完的喁喁情话。可是这一切不能成为现实,而因失望继而失落的怅然心情却如影随形。每当这种时候,主人公就会很自然地想到邻村那个大大咧咧的“傻”姑娘;她是那么“没心没肺”,成天仿佛喝醉酒似的,晕晕乎乎,什么都不放在心上,即便再烦心的事，过一会儿就忘记得一干二净了。

本诗用对比的手法，用邻村“傻”姑娘“幕天席地”的做派来衬托主人公对爱情的执着、难以自拔，后者的单相思更让人想一掬同情之泪。

诗中的“痴醉酒”，笔者没有直接译出来，而是译成simple-minded。因为这仅仅是一个比喻，说明“东姑”的性格：什么都不放在心上，犹如喝醉酒的人。结合后面的“幕天席地了无知”(To whom everything sad will be soon cleanly forgotten)，一位心地单纯的姑娘的形象就凸显出来了。

的信

〔元〕杨维桢

平时诡语难为信，
醉后微言却近真。
昨夜寄将双豆蔻[1]，
始知的的[2]为东邻[3]。

True Love

By Yang Weizhen (the Yuan Dynasty)

His casual joking vows are hard to believe,

But his drunken small talks are close to truth.

Last night he gave me a couple of love flowers,

Which shows his true love for me, I begin to believe.

注释：

①豆蔻：初夏开淡黄色花的多年生草本植物，可入药。在诗文中常常用以比喻少女或象征爱情。

②的的：确确实实。

③东邻：男子心中的美女。语出宋玉《登徒子好色赋》："天下之佳人……莫若臣东家子。"后遂以"东家子"或"东邻子"指美女。

解读与译记：

少男少女由于心理尚不成熟，多半懵懂、善变、随性，其谈恋爱总给人以"过家家"的感觉。本诗里的男孩，由于生性活泼，言谈风趣幽默，常常给深爱他的女孩以不太靠谱的印象。平日在一起的时候，他也许喜欢向女孩子发"毒誓"，说要爱她爱到地老天荒，尽说一些过头话。话说过了头，女孩听起来就觉得是诡语，这就使得女孩感到忐忑不安。但是，当他喝醉酒的时候，又似乎酒后吐真言。从他的话里头能品味出他对女孩的一片真心。有一天晚上，他又突然给女孩送来两支豆蔻花，这使得她猛然觉得，他是真心实意地爱她，而且是时时处处都想着她。诗人将初涉爱河的少男少女那种多变的情感活动和一惊一喜、一疑一信的微妙心态展现得鲜活有趣。

“昨夜寄将双豆蔻”中的“豆蔻”象征少女，也暗指爱情（如南宋陆游《小园春思》中的“小轩愁入丁香结，幽径春生豆蔻梢”）。这里的“双豆蔻”，显然是男孩在向女孩表示自己是真正爱她，暗示他们要永结同心，成百年之好。要是按西方表达爱意的习惯，自然用的是一束玫瑰花。在翻译“双豆蔻”的时候，笔者很踌躇：如果按图索骥地译成 cardamon，势必还要加注，说明在古代中国“豆蔻”可以象征爱情。因此，笔者还是觉得译作 love flowers 来得干净利落。

长干女儿

〔清〕郑　燮

长干[1]女儿年十四，
春游偶过南朝寺。
鬟发纤松拜佛迟，
低头堕下金钗翠[2]。
寺里游人最少年，
闲行拾得翠花钿。
送还不识谁家物，
几嗅香风立怅然。

A Nanjing Maiden

By Zheng Xie (the Qing Dynasty)

A maiden of fourteen, true native of Nanjing,
Happens to enter a temple, sightseeing in spring.
With loosen hair, she is bowing piously to Buddhas
When her gold hairpin falls, her head bending lower.
It so happens that a juvenile's wandering the temple then,
Who quite by chance picks up her lost gold hairpin.
Having tried hard to return it to its owner but he fails,
And he stands still sniffing at its fragrance all at a loss.

注释：

①长干：清朝时南京一条里巷的名字，即长干里。

②金钗翠：与下文的“翠花钿”均为首饰，在诗里指的是同一种头饰，即用金镶玉制成的花色多样的饰品。

解读与译记：

本诗讲述了一对正值豆蔻年华的少年男女失之交臂的故事。

也许是在一个莺歌燕舞、嫩柳垂金的春日午后，趁着外出踏青的机会，善男信女竞相到南京城外的南朝寺里去烧香拜佛。人群里，有位十四岁的女孩，也随大流步入庙内。她也许不像其他香客那样有备而来，只是觉得好玩，赶热闹似的来拜佛。因为年少，贪玩的心思占了上风，外出春游，她不像那些大姑娘，要从头至脚地打扮修饰一番。她匆匆走出家门，连自己的头发也来不及梳理得光整，发上的簪子也没有插好。在跪下拜佛的瞬间，她有些迟疑，虽然模样虔诚，可心里不是十分明白，自己要在佛祖面前许什么愿才好。不经意间，松松的头发上插着的簪子也掉在了地上。

她匆匆起身离开，簪子丢失了竟浑然不知。说来也巧，此时有一位少年也来到佛前，发现了少女失落的簪子。捡到簪子后，他的心里像是被猫抓似的，既兴奋又热切。他既急于将此物送还失主，又想象着，失主一定是一位美女……

"送还不识谁家物，几嗅香风立怅然"，活灵活现地刻画出一位心中爱意萌动的少年，在跟想象中的美少女失之交臂后怅然若失的样子。捡到翠花钿要归还失主，这反映该少年拾金不昧，而想要结识这位素昧平生之人，则是他急于找到她的原动力。失主一时无法找到，他只好伫立四顾，而金钗上留有的少女体香却轻轻袭来，使得他心旌摇曳——期待、心醉、懊丧，五味杂陈！少男少女正情窦初开，其懵懂的情愫、对异性的向往是那么热切、那么纯真！

"鬟发纤松拜佛迟"一句，着重一个"迟"字，可见小女孩心理的不成熟。她不同于成人，拜佛带有极强的功利性：或求财，或求子，或求功名……当她虔诚跪下时，心里却是空白的：不知道在佛祖前求什么才好。笔者译这句的时候，仅凸显她的"虔诚"(piously)。"金钗翠"跟"翠花钿"都指她头上的饰物——金簪子，故译作 gold hairpin 也就可以了。

附：现代爱情诗歌

Appendix: Modern Love Poems

一棵开花的树

席慕蓉

如何让你遇见我
在我最美丽的时刻
为这　我已在佛前　求了五百年
求佛让我们结一段尘缘

佛于是把我化作一棵树
长在你必经的路旁
阳光下慎重地开满了花
朵朵都是我前世的盼望

A Tree in Full Blossom

By Xi Murong

Trying hard to let you meet me
In my prime of beauty, and only for this,
I have been praying to Buddha for five hundred years,
To let us form worldly bonds of affections.

So Buddha has made me become a tree,
And grow on the roadside you'd pass by,
Which is prudently in full blossom in the sun,
And every flower is the hope of my previous life.

当你走近　请你细听

那颤抖的叶是我等待的热情

而当你终于无视地走过

在你身后落了一地的

朋友啊　那不是花瓣

是我凋零的心

When you approach me—oh, just listen carefully

To the quivering leaves, my expectant ardent love,

But finally, when you heedlessly pass it by,

What have fallen behind you on the whole ground,

My dear friends, are not petals of flowers,

But the withered pieces of my broken heart!

解读与译记：

席慕蓉的诗歌，我在学生时代就很喜欢；从她的诗中能看到人们心灵最幽微的地方，听到她对生命朴素而由衷的赞美。至于她的爱情诗，我对《一棵开花的树》情有独钟。

《一棵开花的树》之所以能让我感动，继而难以忘怀，就是因为它拥有对人世间最美好的东西——爱情的悲剧性展示和阐释。

这首爱情诗，“记录”的是一段凄美的单相思！诗中的“我”显然是一位女性，她暗恋着“你”——她心目中的白马王子。为了在自己青春芳华绽放的当口，让她的“白马王子”遇上她，她在佛前竟然整整祈求了五百年！也许是她太过虔诚，佛祖也被她深深地打动了，于是让她转世投胎成一棵树，而且就长在他的必经之地。

她所化身的树，繁花满枝，芬芳四溢，而且每一朵花都开得十分隆重，一如她前世所期盼的那样。这段跨越生死两界的单恋，看起来马上就能功德圆满，可是它的结局却是戴盆望天，令当事人大失所望。

席慕蓉这首诗几乎纯粹用口语写就，没有华丽的辞藻，更无形而上的深奥哲思。它成功的原因，大致可以归结为以下三点。第一，用朴实真挚的感情，站在一位爱情的殉道者——一名可以牺牲时间和生命的姑娘——的立场，去求取一段美好姻缘。第二，为了体现她对爱情的虔诚，竟然让佛祖也参与进来，让其扮演一个“有求必应”的角色。将虚妄当作真实，更突出她的痴迷和执着。第三,诗行和诗节的安排跟“情节”的发展紧密相连:祈求——短暂成功——失败。比如最后四行“而当你终于无视地走过 / 在你身后落了一地的 / 朋友啊 / 那不是花瓣 / 是我凋零的心”里面,诗人将“朋友啊”这一呼告语插在当中,而不是放置于这四句之首——这是他精心的安排。若以“朋友啊”开始,这四行诗就显得平铺直叙,不像目前这样“欲说还休”。同时这语气的突然停顿,似乎在酝酿和积聚感情,把带着血泪的“那不是花瓣 / 是我凋零的心”重重地抛在读者面前。读到这里,整首诗也就戛然而止,读者跟诗中的“我”一起,在经受意外的失落后,承受心灵被扯碎的那种生生的痛!

翻译新诗,的确比翻译古诗词要容易一些。首先是由于现代汉语语法与英语语法有较多相似之处,因此翻译时不用花较多时间去考虑词汇的增补(比如增补主语、动词等)和词序的调整,而且押韵也较为自由;这首诗,甚至连标点符号也没有。但是,新诗往往注重感情起伏和内部节奏的外化,因此在译成英语时,也要十分注意诗行建构跟原诗尽量保持一致。

当然,词汇的翻译也同样要紧扣原诗,既要体现字面意义,又要考虑深层的内涵。比如:“结一段尘缘”(form worldly bonds of affections);“而当你终于无视地走过”(But finally, when you heedlessly pass it by)。后者的“无视”有“漫不经心”“无暇顾及”或“不屑一顾”的含义,将它译作heedlessly,稍许体现“落花有意流水无情”的意味。

沙扬娜拉

（赠日本女郎）

徐志摩

最是那一低头的温柔，

　像一朵水莲花不胜凉风的娇羞，

道一声珍重，道一声珍重，

　那一声珍重里有甜蜜的忧愁——

沙扬娜拉！

Farewell

(*To a Japanese Maiden*)

By Xu Zhimo

What thrills me most is the tenderness shown while you bend your head;
You are as soft and shy as a lotus flower unable to stand a chilly wind.
Take care! Take care of yourself, my dear maiden!

This heartfelt wish has sweet sorrows hidden—

Sayounara (Farewell), my dear maiden!

解读与译记：

徐志摩是“新月派”的领军人物，在中国新诗的产生和完善中，发挥了鼓与呼的作用。他的这首诗是在1924年陪同泰戈尔访问日本时写的，选自以“沙扬娜拉”为题的一组诗，共有十八首；本首是组诗的最后一首。

在陪同泰戈尔访日期间，恰遇日本大地震。当时东京几乎成了废墟一片，景象惨不忍睹。徐志摩亲眼见到日本人民在困难前面所表现出来的勇敢和坚毅，不无感慨地写道：“我们勇敢的邻居们已经交了他们的考卷，他们回答一个干脆的干字。我们不能不佩服。”（《落叶》）也就是在那段时间，他写下了《沙扬娜拉十八首》。这十八首诗，写的是他对日本的总体印象，记录了日本的风土人情。每一首诗都能独自成篇，一如《古诗十九首》。

这首诗可以看作是一首爱情诗。还是一名中学生的时候，我第一次读到它，就被之深深吸引。它甜甜的缠绵、柔婉的旋律，对一名青少年是很有吸引力的。刚开始的时候，我错把“沙扬娜拉”当作这首诗的主人公，后来才知道那是日文“再见”的音译，让自己闹了大笑话，但这也足见徐先生写诗的苦心。看到这个标题，难免觉得这是一位域外妙龄女郎的芳名。凭这标题就赢得了读者的注意力。

徐志摩深受英美现代诗歌的影响，可骨子里他还是一个中国文人。这首诗,很像是从近体诗绝句里演化而来。只要稍加改变,这诗的内涵尽可体现在以下四句诗中:“最是温柔一低头,水莲拂风不胜羞。轻声道别应珍重,半含甜蜜半含愁。”

像“最是那一低头的温柔”这样的句式,在我们的古诗里经常会读到,比如“最是湖东行不足”(唐代白居易《钱塘湖春行》)等。在翻译这句诗时,笔者首先想到的是,应该怎样展示她低下头去的刹那,给人以羞涩和妩媚的印象。因此这里译作What thrills me most is the tenderness shown while you bend your head。用动词thrill来传达诗人见到她低下头去的瞬间所显露的难以言状的女性美,使人偶然一瞥就怦然心动。“像一朵水莲花不胜凉风的娇羞”(You are as soft and shy as a lotus flower unable to stand a chilly wind)。“娇羞”译作soft and shy,既切近原义,又运用了头韵的修辞法。将“那一声珍重里有甜蜜的忧愁——”中的“一声珍重”译作this heartfelt wish,旨在增强take care of yourself所表达情感的真挚程度,表明这种道别之声来自心灵深处的真情实感。如果将“有”译作with或have,语气就不够强烈,故将这一行诗译成了This heartfelt wish has sweet sorrows hidden—。hidden一词,既能表达“深藏”或“包含”,又很自然地跟前一句中的maiden押韵,一举两得。

偶 然

徐志摩

我是天空里的一片云，
偶尔投影在你的波心——
　你不必讶异，
　更无须欢喜——
在转瞬间消灭了踪影。

你我相逢在黑夜的海上，
你有你的，我有我的，方向；
　你记得也好，
　最好你忘掉，
在这交会时互放的光亮！

Chance Meeting

By Xu Zhimo

I'm a floating cloud in the sky,

Casting my shadow on your heart of ripples.

  Don't be surprised,

  Nor need to be pleased,

In a wink, I'll disappear without trace.

You and I meet in the sea at night;

You have your direction, and I have mine.

  You may as well remember

  Or had better forget

This brilliance jointly made by us two while meeting.

解读与译记：

人世间有许多机缘巧合，使得风云变幻，人力难以驾驭。所谓机缘，是一种或然性，真切地发生在生活当中。徐志摩这首《偶然》，就是因爱情的擦肩而过而发出的慨叹。

我们在谈论某对青年男女之间的婚姻是否会成功的时候，往往会说："这要看缘分了。"诗中的"偶然"，也就是所谓"缘分"。

诗的第一节里，诗人把天上云影投射在湖中的波心比作"机缘"。这的确是千载难逢的事，不像"天光云影共徘徊"，常常能看得见、遇得着。突发事件让人惊喜，可是诗人提醒我们不要太过乐观，这种偶发之事也许会像昙花一现，转瞬即逝。

在第二节中，诗人把人与人之间的邂逅，比作大海上两艘轮船探照灯光束的交汇。这种事件发生的概率更是小之又小，所以更值得铭记与珍惜。何况光束交汇的一刹那所释放的光辉明亮炫目，让人久久难以忘怀。可是诗人却故作豁达，宕开一笔："你记得也好，/ 最好你忘掉，/ 在这交会时互放的光亮！"诗人这种欲擒故纵的写法，更显得他对机缘巧合的在乎和珍惜。

诗人把男女间的邂逅当作"缘分"，这在中国的传统文化中，会获得很广泛的认同。但是，这也并非完全否定人的积极性和主动性。诗人这种从反面着墨的手法，更显得他对爱情的执着和痴迷。

在《偶然》中,诗人吸收了西方诗歌中的一些句法,作为丰富和完善中国新诗的借鉴。比如:“你有你的,我有我的,方向”;“你记得也好,/ 最好你忘掉”。这些句型对中国新诗的建构具有积极的作用。

雨　巷

戴望舒

撑着油纸伞，独自
彷徨在悠长，悠长
又寂寥的雨巷，
我希望逢着
一个丁香一样地
结着愁怨的姑娘。

她是有
丁香一样的颜色，
丁香一样的芬芳，

A Lane in the Rain

By Dai Wangshu

Under an oil-paper umbrella, all alone,

I'm padding along a long, long

And desolate lane in the rain,

Longing for coming across

A maiden like a clove flower,

Weighed down with anxiety.

She is possessed of

The same color as a clove flower,

The same fragrance as a clove flower,

丁香一样的忧愁,
在雨中哀怨,
哀怨又彷徨;

她彷徨在这寂寥的雨巷,
撑着油纸伞
像我一样,
像我一样地
默默彳亍着,
冷漠,凄清,又惆怅。

她静默地走近
走近,又投出
太息一般的眼光,
她飘过

The same anxiety as a clove flower,

Resentful in the rain,

And hesitant as well;

She's padding hesitantly

Along the lonely lane in the rain,

Under an oil-paper umbrella like mine,

As what I'm doing:

Solitarily walking, quiet,

Indifferent, cheerless and melancholy.

Gently she's approaching me,

Closer, and casting

A glance like a deep sigh;

She's drifting

像梦一般地，
像梦一般地凄婉迷茫。

像梦中飘过
一枝丁香地，
我身旁飘过这女郎；
她静默地远了，远了，
到了颓圮的篱墙，
走尽这雨巷。

在雨的哀曲里，
消了她的颜色，
散了她的芬芳，
消散了，甚至她的
太息般的眼光，

As in a dream,

A dream, sorrowful and confused.

As in a dream,

This maiden's drifting by me

Like a clove flower;

She's leaving me silently farther and farther

Till she comes to the crumbled wall,

The end of the lane in the rain.

In the doleful tune of the rain,

Her color is fading

And her fragrance being dissipated:

All's disappearing, even

Her glance like a sigh

丁香般的惆怅。

撑着油纸伞，独自
彷徨在悠长，悠长
又寂寥的雨巷，
我希望飘过
一个丁香一样地
结着愁怨的姑娘。

And her melancholy of a clove flower.

Under an oil-paper umbrella, all alone,
I'm padding along a long, long
And desolate lane in the rain,
Longing for seeing
A maiden, drifting like a clove flower,
Weighed down with anxiety.

解读与译记：

《戴望舒诗集》在20世纪80年代初由四川人民出版社印刷发行时，大学生们争相购买。那时离诗人戴望舒逝世已经有约三十个年头了。同学们知道他是一位现代派诗人；他写的《雨巷》一诗，在学生当中广为流传，许多人称他为“雨巷诗人”。

一位撑着油纸伞的年轻女孩，在雨中的小巷里踽踽独行，脸上是一抹惆怅……不要说诗人望舒先生，换成谁都会有瞥上一眼的冲动，也许受好奇心的驱使，想琢磨出个究竟来。

《雨巷》采用了中心意象“丁香”，很可能受到五代李璟的《摊破浣溪沙（手卷真珠上玉钩）》中“青鸟不传云外信，丁香空结雨中愁”诗句的启迪。望舒先生只是将雨中包着丁香结的意象，从亡国之君李璟身上挪移到一个身份不明的姑娘头上，意象的指向更加模糊，意境也就更为开阔。这就使得读者对“她”身份的揭晓更感兴趣。一直读到诗的末尾，诗人始终没有揭开结着愁怨的姑娘的真实身份。这就是诗人的高明之处。诗歌，特别是抒情诗，它所展示的是一片朦胧的意境，抑或一个难以猜中的谜语，一百个读者可以有一百种解读。

这首诗很有章法：一共七个诗节，首尾两个诗节基本相同，每节六行，每行音节数量不等，但总的说来很少有超过四个音节的，在适当的地方押韵（ang）。这样的外在结构，读起来舒缓流畅，用来表达淡淡的忧伤，非常适合。

这首《雨巷》可能是望舒先生的早期作品，整首诗很有乐感。因为在他的《诗论零札》中他曾这样表示："诗的韵律不在字的抑扬顿挫上，而是在诗的情绪的抑扬顿挫上，即在诗情的程度上。"这表明写这条札记的时候，他的诗风正从倾向于浪漫主义朝着现代主义转变。

翻译《雨巷》的时候，虽然很难做到有原诗那样的乐感，但译者尽自己的努力在诗行的重建上做些努力，比如"撑着油纸伞，独自 / 彷徨在悠长，悠长 / 又寂寥的雨巷"（Under an oil-paper umbrella, all alone, / I'm padding along a long, long / And desolate lane in the rain）。意象的翻译也紧靠原作，比如"一个丁香一样地 / 结着愁怨的姑娘"（A maiden like a clove flower, / Weighed down with anxiety）。翻译回来，就是"一个像丁香一样，愁肠百结的姑娘"。

致橡树

舒 婷

我如果爱你——

绝不像攀援的凌霄花，

借你的高枝炫耀自己；

我如果爱你——

绝不学痴情的鸟儿，

为绿荫重复单调的歌曲；

也不止像泉源，

常年送来清凉的慰藉；

也不止像险峰，

增加你的高度，衬托你的威仪。

To the Oak

By Shu Ting

If I love you—
I'll never be like the climbing Chinese trumpet creeper,
Which shows off its height in dependence on your high branches;
If I love you—
I'll never mimic the obsessed bird,
Who repeats the simple tune for the green shade of trees;
Nor will I only be like the fountainhead,
Which brings you cool comfort all the year round;
Nor will I only be like the perilous peak,
Which helps you become higher, or set off your bearing;

甚至日光。

甚至春雨。

不,这些都还不够!

我必须是你近旁的一株木棉,

作为树的形象和你站在一起。

根,紧握在地下;

叶,相触在云里。

每一阵风过,

我们都相互致意,

但没有人

听懂我们的言语。

你有你的铜枝铁干

像刀,像剑,

也像戟;

我有我红硕的花朵,

Nor the sunlight,

Nor the spring rain,

No! All this is not yet enough!

I will be a kapok growing close to you,

Standing side by side with you as a true tree:

Our roots hold each other tight in the earth,

And our leaves touch each other in the clouds.

Whenever there's a wind by us,

We'll salute each other;

But nobody knows

What we're talking about.

You have your branches as if made of iron and bronze,

Which are like knives, swords

And also halberds;

I have big red flowers

像沉重的叹息，

又像英勇的火炬。

我们分担寒潮、风雷、霹雳；

我们共享雾霭、流岚、虹霓，

仿佛永远分离，

却又终身相依。

这才是伟大的爱情，

坚贞就在这里：

爱——

不仅爱你伟岸的身躯，

也爱你坚持的位置，

足下的土地。

Which resemble a heavy sigh,

And a brave torch, too.

We share the same cold wave, storm and bolt;

We share the same morning fog, floating mist and rainbow.

We seem as if ever separated though,

We are dependent on each other for life.

That is our great, constant love

herein:

For love,

I love your tall, sturdy stature,

And also the place you stick to,

And the soil underfoot!

解读与译记：

20世纪七八十年代，《致橡树》这首诗红遍大江南北，女诗人舒婷的名字也不胫而走，大有“天下谁人不识君”的味道。

照舒婷自己说，这首爱情诗的发端是她在鼓浪屿跟某位老诗人的一次闲聊。这位老诗人说，他一生认识的女性不少，但真正能在他脑子里留下较深印象的，真叫凤毛麟角。他评价女同胞时，言辞犀利、刻薄，大男子主义溢于言表。舒婷对这位诗人的言辞不以为然，她想，难道在女人眼里，个个男人都会是十全十美的吗？她是这样认为的：“花和蝶的关系是相悦，木和水的关系是互需，只有一棵树才能感受到另一棵树的体验，感受鸟儿、阳光、春雨的给予。”（《凹凸手记》）那天晚上，她夜不成寐，奋笔疾书，写下了《致橡树》。

许多人称舒婷为朦胧诗的代表人物。可是，在笔者看来，《致橡树》一点也不朦胧。它是一首吸收了传统咏物诗的手法用来抒写现代爱情的诗歌。无论是对橡树、木棉、凌霄花的形象，还是对它们所具的生物学特征，读者几乎一眼就能“对号入座”地做出解读，没有一丁点儿的模糊，更说不上朦胧。不过，在当时的社会认知背景下，舒婷能提出这样态度鲜明的爱情观，实在难能可贵。更值得一提的是，她把个人的爱情放在了爱祖国、爱人民的大背景中去审视，让人称道。“不仅爱你伟岸的身躯，/ 也爱你坚持的位置，/ 足下的土地。”（I love your tall, sturdy stature, / And also the place you stick to / And the soil underfoot!）笔者在这里重复使用love一词，以表示强调：平等的男欢女爱固然重要，但个人的爱情总离不开爱国家、爱民族这种大爱情怀的支撑。